WHO AM I?
WHAT AM I?

Through countless accidents that would have killed another man, Paul had survived. His intuition told him it was more than luck— but his questioning brought forth no answers, only more questions.

Was he a super-being, immune to physical laws? Was he dead and living in another man's body? Had he been given this mysterious power of survival for a purpose?

His journey toward understanding takes him through many strange byways, as well as the secret labyrinths of his own identity....

NO ROOM FOR MAN

(Original title: Necromancer)

GORDON·R. DICKSON

MANOR
BOOKS
INC.

A MANOR BOOK

First printing .... September, 1963
Second printing .... December, 1966
Third printing .... November, 1972
Fourth printing .... November, 1974

Manor Books Inc.
329 Fifth Avenue
New York, New York 10016

Library of Congress Catalog Card Number: 62-11444

Book One: ISOLATE

> *And now, through double glass, I see*
> *My brother's image, darklingly.*
> *Now, aid us, Thor, who prisoners be.*
> *Come*—hammer, *Lord! And set us free.*
>
> THE ENCHANTED TOWER

Chapter 1

The mine, generally speaking, was automatic. It consisted of some hundred and eighty million dollars' worth of equipment, spread out through three and a half cubic miles of gold-ore-bearing rock—granite and quartz—all controlled by the single console where the shift engineer on duty sat.

Like some ponderous, many-purposed organism, the mine walked in the layered rock. On various levels it gnawed out the gold-bearing ore, ground it up to pebble-sized chunks, and sent it by the carload up six hundred feet or more to the open air and the equipment above. As the mine machinery moved, it created and abandoned surface shafts, elevator tubes, new exploratory levels and stopes; and extended the vast central cavern through which the heavier machinery and its controlling console slid with the work in progress, laying down rails before and taking them up behind.

The single engineer on shift at the time controlled all this. And a touch of megalomania did him no harm on the job. He was seated before the control panels of the console like the identity before the brain. His job was the job of ultimate control. Logical decision, and the facts on which to base decision were supplied by the computer element in the equipment. The logically optimum answer was available at the touch of a button. But it had been discovered that, like the process of living itself, there was more to modern mining than logic.

The best engineers had *feel*. It was a sensitivity born of experience, of talent, and even of something like love, with which they commanded, not only the mountains, but the machine they rode and directed.

Now this too was added to the list of man's endeavors for which some special talent was needed. Less than ten per cent of the young mining engineers graduating every year turned out to have the necessary extra ability to become one with the titan they directed. Even in the twenty-first century's overcrowded employment marts, mines were continually on the hunt for more shift engineers. Even four hours at a time, and even for the talented ten per cent, was a long time to be the faultless god in the machine. And the machinery never rested.

Six hundred feet overhead of the man at the console, Paul Formain, on his first morning at Malabar Mine, stepped from his small individual quarters of white bubble plastic, and saw the mountains.

And suddenly, there it was again, as it had been time and again since his boating accident of five years before, and had been more recently, lately.

But it was not now the open sea that he saw. Or even the dreamlike image of a strange, shadowy figure in some sort of cape and a high-peaked hat, who had seemed to bring him back to life after he had died in the boat, and returned him to the boat to be finally found and rescued by the coast guard.

This time, it was the mountains.

Suddenly, turning from the white, plastic door, he stopped and saw them. Around him was a steep slope with the other white buildings of the Malabar Mine. Above him the fragile blue of a spring sky spoke to the dark blue of the deep lake below, which filled this cleft in the mountain rock. About him in every direction were the

Canadian Rockies, stretching thirty miles in one direction to the British Columbia city of Kamloops, in the other to the Coast Range and the stony beaches touching the salt Pacific Ocean surf. Unexpectedly, he felt them.

Like kings they stood up around him, the mountains. The surf sounded in his blood, and abruptly he was growing, striding to meet them. He was mountain-size with the mountains. With them, he felt the eternal movement of the earth. For a moment he was naked but unshaken to the winds of understanding. And they blew to him one word:

Fear.

Do not go down into the mine.

". . . You will get over this, this sort of thing," the psychiatrist in San Diego had assured him, five years before, after the accident. "Now that you've worked it out for yourself and understand it."

"Yes," said Paul.

It had made sense then, the way he had explained it to himself under the psychiatrist's guidance. He was an orphan, since the time of his parents' simultaneous deaths in a transportation accident, when he was nine. He had been assigned to good foster parents, but they were not the same. He had always been solitary.

He had lacked what the San Diego psychiatrist called "protective selfishness." He had the knack of understanding people without the usual small urge to turn this understanding to his own advantage. It had embarrassed those who might have been his friends, once they understood this capability in him. They had an instinctive urge to put a protective distance between himself and them. Underneath, they feared his knowledge and did not trust his restraint. As a boy he felt their withdrawal without understanding the reasons behind it. And this, said the psychiatrist, gave him a false picture of his own situation.

". . . After all," said the psychiatrist, "this lack of a desire to take advantage of a capability, amounted to a disability. But no worse than any other disability, such

as blindness or loss of a limb. There was no need to feel
that you could not live with it."

But that was the way, it seemed, that unconsciously
he had felt. And that feeling had culminated in an unconscious attempt at suicide.

". . . There's no doubt," said the psychiatrist, "that
you got the bad-weather, small-craft warning put out by
the coast guard. Or that you knew you were dangerously
far offshore for any weather, in such a light sailboat."

So the storm had driven him out to sea and lost him.
He had been adrift, and in the still days following, death
had come like some heavy gray bird to sit perched on the
idle mast, waiting.

". . . You were in a condition for hallucination," said
the psychiatrist. "It was natural to imagine you had already died. Then, when afterward you were rescued, you
automatically searched for some justification of the fact
that you were still alive. Your unconscious provided this
fantasy of having been brought back to life by a father-
like figure, tall and mysterious, and wrapped in the gar-
ments that denote magical ability. But when you had
fully recovered, your conscious mind could not help
finding this story somewhat thin."

No, thought Paul, it couldn't help thinking so. He remembered, in the San Diego hospital, lying there and
doubting the whole memory.

"So to bolster it, you produced these moments of extreme, almost painful sensitivity. Which filled two needs.
They provided support for your delirium fantasy of having been raised from the dead, and they acted as an excuse for what had caused the death-wish in the first
place. Unconsciously you were telling yourself that you
were not crippled, but 'different.' "

"Yes," Paul had said at that point. "I see."

"Now that you've dug out the true situation for yourself, the need for justification should diminish. The
fantasy should fade and the sensitivity moments grow
less frequent, until they disappear."

"That's good to hear," said Paul.

Only, in the past five years the moments had not
dwindled and disappeared. They had stayed with him, as
the original dream had stuck stubbornly in the back of

his mind. He thought of seeing another psychiatrist, but then the thought would come that the first had done him no good at all. So what was there to expect from a second?

Instead, in order to live with his problem, he had anchored himself to something that he had discovered in himself since the accident. Deep within him now, something invincible stood four-square to the frequent gusts from the winds of feeling. Somehow he thought of it as being connected to, but independent of, the dream magician in the tall hat. So when, as now, the winds blew warnings, he felt them without being driven by them.

Fear: said the mountains. *Do not go down into the mine.*

That's foolish, said Paul's conscious mind. It reminded him that he was at last hired for the work to which all his education had pointed him. To a job that in the present overcrowded world was the dream of many and the achievement of few. He reached for that which stood unconquerable in the back of his mind.

Fear, it replied, is merely one more in the multitude of factors to be taken into account in moving from point *A* to point *B*.

Paul shook himself free from the winds of feeling, back to the ordinary existence of the world. The buildings of the Malabar Mine were all around him. A little distance down the slope from where he stood the wife of the company auditor came out on her back step and called something across a small white fence to the wife of the surface engineer in the yard adjoining. It was Paul's first day on the job and already he was close to being overdue on the job underground. He turned his gaze from the mountains and the buildings, to the near concrete walk leading to the main shaft head of the mine. And headed toward it, and the waiting skip.

Chapter 2

The skip slid Paul down some six hundred steeply slanting feet through mountain stone. For all the romanticism of its old-fashioned name, it was nothing more in fact than a magnetic tube elevator. Through the transparent walls of the tube, granite and rose quartz flickered at him as he descended. They spoke to him as the mountains had, but in smaller voices, fine, thin, crystalline voices with no yield, no kindness to them, and no mercy. Between them and himself, Paul's own faint image in the tube wall kept pace with his descent—it was the image of a square-shouldered young man of twenty-three, already past any look of boyishness or youth.

He was large-boned and tall, strong-featured, round-headed, and athletic-looking. A football-player type, but not one of the game's commoner varieties. He was not bulky enough for a lineman, not tense enough for the backfield. End—that was the sort of position he fitted. And, strongly calm, with long-fingered capable hands to catch the ball, he remembered playing it well. That had been on the first team at Colorado Institute of Mines, where he had taken his undergraduate work.

His eyes were curiously deep, and a warm, gray color. His mouth was thin-lipped, but a little wide and altogether friendly. His light, straight brown hair was already receding at the temples. He wore it clipped short, and he would be nearly bald before his thirties were out, but since he was not the sort of man to whom good looks are necessary, this would make little difference.

He looked instinctively in command of things. Strongly male, intelligent, physically large and strong, with a knack for doing things right the first time around. And he was all these things. It was only when people got to know him intimately that they saw past to the more complex inner part of him, the part where his own very different image of himself was kept. There were moments like this, as he suddenly caught sight of his outer self mirrored

10

somewhere, when Paul was as startled as if he had come face to face with some stranger.

The skip stopped at Dig Level.

Paul stepped out into a bright, huge cavern filled to its lofty ceiling with the bright metal of equipment mounted ponderously on rails. The acid-damp air of below-ground struck coolly into his lungs, and the atmosphere of the mine seemed to flow into and through him as he walked down alongside the crusher to the small cleared space that surrounded the console. There, seated upon the rails, was the console itself. And at it—at the keys and stops that resembled nothing so much as the keyboard of some huge electronic organ, with the exception of the several small viewing tanks in the console's very center—a small, round-bodied, black-haired man in his forties sat winding up the duties of the shift he was just ending.

Paul came up to the edge of the platform on which the console and its operator sat.

"Hi," he said.

The other man glanced down.

"I'm the new man--Paul Formain," said Paul. "Ready for relief?"

The departing engineer made several quick motions about the console, his short, thick fingers active. He leaned back in the control seat, then stretched. He stood up to turn a tough, friendly face toward Paul.

"Paul?" he asked. "What was the last name?"

"Formain. Paul Formain."

"Right. Pat Teasely." He held out a small, square hand with a good deal of strength in its grip.

They shook. Teasely's accent was Australian—that particular accent which Australians are continually infuriated to have called cockney by inexperienced North Americans. He gave forth a personality that was as plain and straightforward as common earth. It touched soothingly against Paul, after the violence of the mountains.

"Looks like a nice clear dig for your first shift," Teasely said. "Judging by the cores."

"Sounds good," replied Paul.

"Right. No large faults in sight and the vein drift's less than eight degrees off the vertical. Watch for crowding on the ore trains going up Number One surface shaft, though."

"Oh?" said Paul. "Bug in the works?"

"Not really. They've been jackknifing and getting jammed just above Number Eight hatch, about sixty feet short of exit. The shaft's cut a little small; but no point in widening it when we'll be driving a new one in about a hundred and fifty hours. I've been up twice this last shift, though, to kick a car back on the tracks."

"All right," said Paul. "Thanks." He stepped past Teasely and sat down at the console. He looked up at the smaller man. "See you topside at the bar this evening, perhaps?"

"Might." Teasely lingered. His blunt face looked down, uncompromising, individualistic, and congenial. "You out of one of the American colleges?"

"Colorado."

"Wife and family along?"

Paul shook his head. His fingers were already moving about, becoming acquainted with the console.

"No," he said. "I'm a bachelor—and an orphan."

"Come have dinner at our place then, sometime," said Teasely. "I've got the sort of wife likes to cook for guests."

"Thanks," said Paul. "I'll do that."

"See you."

Paul heard Teasely's footsteps crunch away in the loose rubble of the cavern floor. He went back to the controls, and ran through his take-over check list. It took him about six minutes. When that was done he knew the position of every piece of equipment and how it was behaving. Then he turned to the programing section and ran a four-hour estimate and forecast.

It checked with Teasely's estimate. A routine, easy shift. For a moment he laid his fingers on the gross control tabs of the computer override and sought for the individual qualities of the machine through the little working vibrations that reached him through his finger tips. A sensation of blind, purposeful, and irresistible force at work was returned to him; like, but not identical with, the feel of all other mine controls he had touched before. He took his hands away.

For the moment, he had nothing to do. He leaned back in his bucket seat at the console and thought about leaving things here for a look at the surface shaft where Teasely had reported the ore cars had occasionally been getting stuck. He decided against it. It was best to stick close to the console until he had built up a familiarity with this new mine.

The little lights and gauges and small viewing screens showed their flickers of color and movement normally before him. He reached over and switched a Vancouver news broadcast onto the screen of his central viewing tank.

Abruptly, he looked down as if from a window onto the plaza entrance to the Koh-i-Nor Hotel, at Chicago Complex. He recognized the location—it was a hotel he had stayed at once or twice himself when he was in the Chicago area. As he looked down on it now, he saw a small knot of people carrying the cameras and equipment of reporters, gathered around three people. The view zoomed in for a shot from an apparent distance of only a few feet and Paul had a second's close-up glimpse of two of the three, who were standing a little back from the third. The two were a flat-bodied, crop-haired man of middle age, and a tall, slim girl of Paul's age, whose appearance jerked suddenly at Paul's attention before the camera moved away from her, and left him frowning over what could have seemed so remarkable about her. He had never seen either her or the flat-bodied man before.

But then he forgot about her. For the third member of the group was filling the screen. And there was something about him that would have held any viewer's attention.

He was a gaunt giant of an old man in the formal black-and-white of evening clothes. Very stark and somber in these, he bent his head a little to avoid the low edge of a candy-striped beach umbrella overhead. And, although straight enough for the years he seemed to own, he leaned heavily on the carved handle of a thick cane in his right hand. The motion spread his wide shoulders, so that he seemed to stoop above the crowd of reporters. Dark glasses obscured the expression around his eyes—but even without these, his face was an enigma. Though it stood clear and sharp on the screen before him, Paul could not seem to grasp its image as a whole. It was a collection of features, but there was no totality to it. Paul found himself staring at the straight lips and the deep parentheses of creases around the corners of the mouth as the man spoke.

". . . robes?" one of the newspeople was just finishing asking.

The lips smiled.

"You wouldn't expect a mechanic to go out to dinner in his working clothes, now would you?" The voice from the lips was deep and pleasantly sardonic. "If you people want to see me in my official robes, you'll have to make an appointment to meet me during my office hours."

"Do they have office hours in the Chantry Guild, Mr. Guildmaster?" asked another reporter. There was laughter, but not disrespectful laughter. The lips smiled with them.

"Come and find out," said the lips. Paul frowned. A small closed pocket in his memory had opened up. He had heard of the Chantry Guild—or Société Chanterie. Come to think of it, he had heard of them now and again—quite often, in fact. They were a cult group—devil-worshipers, or some such. He had always dismissed them as a group of crackpots. But this man—this Guildmaster—was nothing so simple as a crackpot. He was . . .

Frustrated, Paul put his fingers instinctively out to the image of the man before him. But the cold glassy surface of the screen baffled his finger tips. The reporters were still asking questions.

"What about Operation Springboard, Mr. Guildmaster?"

The lips quirked.

"What about it?"

"Is the Guild against an attempt to reach the nearer stars?"

"Well now, ladies and gentlemen . . ." The lips smiled. "What did the Sumerian and Semite say in the days of the older gods? I believe they called the planets *sheep that are far away*.' Did they not? Shamash and

Adad were the deities responsible for that statement, as you can find by checking your ancient histories. And if habitable worlds are like sheep, then surely there must be a great many strayed around farther stars which we can find again."

And the smile stayed on the lips.

"Then the Guild is in favor of the station on Mercury? You don't object to work on methods for interstellar travel?"

"Such," said the lips, and the smile vanished, "is not my concern, or the concern of the Guild. Man may play with the technical toys and sciences as he has in the past; he may play with space and the stars. But it will only sicken him further, as it has already sickened him almost to his end. There is only one thing that concerns us of the Guild and that's the destruction that will save Man from himself."

"Mr. Guildmaster," said a voice, "you can't mean total——"

"Total and absolute!" The deep voice strengthened in the speaker. "Complete. Destruction. The destruction of Man and all his works." The voice grew, sonorously near to chanting, on a note that sent a sudden wild surge of feeling through Paul, like a powerful shock from a vein-injected stimulant. "There have been forces at work for eight hundred years that would save Man from his destruction. Woe to Man when that day comes, that he is safe and saved. Woe to Woman and children unborn, when the last strength to destroy himself is finally stolen from him. For by his own eternal life will he be doomed, and only by his destruction may he survive."

The buzzing of an alarm signaled the sudden jackknifing and jamming of an ore train in surface tube A. Paul's hand went out automatically and slapped a fifteen-minute break on shaft power.

"And so I charge you"—the voice rolled like drums below a guillotine from the screen before him—"that you look to the welfare of man and not to yourselves. That you turn your backs on the false promise of life and face the reality of death. That you charge yourselves with a duty. And that duty is complete—is utter—is total destruction. Destruction. Destruction! *Destruction. . . .*"

Paul blinked and sat up.

The mine was all around him. The console was before him and in its center screen the group on the plaza of the Koh-i-Nor was breaking up. The newspeople were dispersing. The old man and the girl and man with him were following a fourth man—a thin young man with black hair and a tense, driving walk—into the hotel. Paul stared. He felt that only a minute had gone by, but even that was startling. For one of the peculiar facts about him was that he was completely unresponsive to hypnosis. It was a trait that had complicated matters for the psychiatrist who had worked with him following the boating accident. How, then, could he have lost even a minute?

Sudden memory of the jackknifed cars in the surface tube broke him away from his personal puzzle. A more general power shutoff of equipment would be required unless he could solve that problem shortly. He left the console and took the chain lift alongside surface shaft Number One. The telltale on the console had spotted the jam-up at a hundred and forty-three feet below the shaft mouth. He reached Number Eight trouble hatch, turned on the lights in the shaft, and crawled through into the shaft himself. He saw the trouble, almost directly before him.

The Number One surface shaft, like the skip tube, approached the surface from the mine below at an angle of roughly sixty degrees. A single powered rail ran up the bottom center of the shaft, and the fat-bodied, open-topped ore cars, filled with pebble-sized rock from below, rolled their cogwheels up the cleated rail. The cleats themselves served Paul now as hand and footholds as he climbed up to where one of the cars sat off the rail, angled against the stony wall.

Still wondering about the familiar-looking girl and the extraordinary cultist who called himself the Guildmaster, Paul braced himself against the sharp-pointed wall of the shaft and the last car. He kicked at the hitch between the two cars. On the third kick, the hitch suddenly unbound the kink it had acquired when the car had jackknifed.

With a snap and a grunt from the stored power in the motorized base of each car, the train suddenly straightened out.

As it did, the lights in the shaft dimmed, then flashed up again without warning as all the motors in all the cars hummed steadily to life. The train jerked and moved up the shaft, and without thinking, instinctively, Paul leaped and clung to the final car of the train.

It burst on him then, brilliantly as mountains seen suddenly against a high spring sky, that in his preoccupation with the news broadcast he had only put a temporary fifteen-minute hold on power to the shaft. And afterward, following his little blackout, he had omitted to set the power controls for the shaft on manual.

Now he was being carried up the shaft by the last car in the train. A few inches below him, the powered rail promised instant electrocution if he touched it. And the high-sided cars, all but filling the shaft, would block any try he could make to open the emergency hatches yet between him and the surface, as the train passed them.

The walls and the roof were close.

The roof in particular pressed down near to him. Rough-chewed from the granite and quartz, it rose and dipped unevenly. At points along the shaft, Paul knew, it would all but scrape the tops of the ore cars. If he could keep low, he might be able to ride the car he was holding to, to the surface. But, clinging to the back of it as he was, he felt his grip weakening.

He pulled himself upward, flat onto the bed of ore in the car. The roof under which he was passing scraped harshly against the back of his head as the ore train, leaving the lighted section where he had put it back on the track, plunged upward into darkness. His hands pawing at the small sharp rock in the car, Paul dug furiously, burrowing himself in. Swaying and rumbling, the train climbed on. In the blackness Paul did not even see ahead the low point of the roof that was approaching. . . .

Out in the clear mountain morning the surface engineer on duty had been drawn to the mouth of the Number One shaft by the blinking of a white trouble light on his own console, and a later automatic signal that power to that shaft had been cut. He had come to the shaft mouth, only to be joined a few minutes later by the managing engineer, who had been keeping his eye on the telltales in his office, this day with a new man underground for the first time.

"There it goes," said the surface engineer, a slight man named Diego and as young as Paul, as the hum of motors echoed once more up the natural speaking tube of the shaft. "He got it fixed."

"A little slow," said the Malabar mine manager. He frowned. "Let's wait a minute here and see what the trouble was."

They waited. The humming and the clank of the cogwheels approached. The first car poked its front out into the sunlight and leveled off on the flat.

"What's that?" asked the mine manager, suddenly. There was a shadowy outline visible in the gloom around the approaching final car.

The train trundled automatically on. The last car emerged into the sunlight and the bright illumination fell full on the shape of a man, half-buried and unmoving in the load of ore.

"My God!" said the mine manager. "Stop those cars and help me get him off there!"

But the young surface engineer was already being sick, turned away and leaning against the millhouse wall, in the early shadow of the mountains.

Chapter 3

The clerk working the afternoon division, day shift, on the room desk of the Koh-i-Nor Hotel in the downtown area of the Chicago Complex, was conscious of the fact that his aptitude tests had determined that he should find work in a particular class of job. The class was that of ornament—actually unnecessary from the point of view of modern hotel equipment. Accordingly he worked conscientiously at the primary virtue of a good ornament—being as hard to overlook as possible.

He did not look up when he heard footsteps approach his desk and stop before it. He continued to write in elegant longhand at the list of currently newsworthy guests he was making on a bulletin sheet laid down beside the guest register.

"I have a reservation," said a man's voice. "Paul Formain."

"Very good," said the clerk, adding another name to his list without looking up. He paused to admire the smooth, flowing loops in the *p's* and *l's* of his penmanship.

Abruptly, he felt his hand caught and held by a fist considerably larger than his own. It checked his pen's movement. The strange grasp held his hand like an imprisoned fly—not crushingly, but with a hint of unyielding power in reserve. Startled, a little scared, the clerk looked up.

He found himself facing a tall young-old man with only one arm, the hand of which was holding him with such casual power.

"Sir?" said the clerk. His voice pitched itself a little higher than he would have preferred.

"I said," said the tall man, patiently, "I have a reservation. Paul Formain."

"Yes sir. Of course." Once more the clerk made an effort to free his trapped hand. As if by an afterthought, the tall man let go. The clerk turned hurriedly to his desk register and punched out the name. The register lighted up with information. "Yes sir. Here it is. An outside single. What décor?"

"Modern."

"Of course, Mr. Formain. Room 1412. Elevators around the corner to your left. I'll see your luggage is delivered to you immediately it arrives. Thank you. . . ."

But the tall, one-armed man had already gone off toward the elevators. The clerk looked after him, and then down at his own right hand. He moved the fingers of it experimentally. It had never before occurred to him what wonderfully engineered things those fingers were.

Up in room 1412 Paul stripped and showered. By the time he stepped out of the shower, his single suitcase had emerged from the luggage-delivery chute in the wall of the room. Half-dressed, he caught sight of himself in the mirror, which gave back his lean, flat-muscled image wearing the gray-green disposable slacks he had pressed for from the room dispenser after the shower. Above the waistband of the slacks, his chest and shoulders showed a healthy tan. The fine scars left by the plastic surgery had now faded almost to the point of invisibility. It was eight months since the accident in the mine, early in a new spring, with gray skies and a March wind blowing chilly off Lake Michigan.

The stub of his left arm looked shrunken. Not so much, it seemed, because it no longer had the rest of the limb to support, but in contrast to the right arm that remained to him.

The compensation development of the right arm had proceeded with unusual speed and to extremes, according to Paul's physicians. It hung now, reflected in the mirror's surface, like a great, living club of bone and muscle. The deltoid humped up like a rock over the point where clavicle toed into shoulder frame; and from the lower part of the deltoid, triceps and biceps humped like whale-backs down to the smaller, knot-like muscles above the elbow. Below the elbow, the flexors and the brachioradialis rose like low hills. The thenar group was a hard lump at the base of his thumb.

And it was as a club that he sometimes thought of it. No—nothing so clumsy as a club. Like some irresistible, battering-ram force made manifest in flesh and skeleton. In the three-quarters of a year since the mine accident, through the long process of hospitalization, operation, and recuperation, that invincible part of him which sat in the back of his mind seemed to have chosen the arm for itself. The arm was *that* part of Paul, the part that doubted nothing, and least of all itself. Nor had time to waste on the posing of a hotel clerk.

Obscurely, it bothered Paul. Like a man testing a sore tooth continually with a tongue, he found himself frequently trying the arm's strength on things, and being disturbed anew each time by the result. Now, standing before the mirror, he reached out and closed his hand around the single ornament in the starkly modern hotel room—a tulip-shaped pewter vase about nine inches high, with a single red rose in it, that had been sitting on the dresser top. The vase fitted easily into his grasp, and he lifted it, slowly tightening the grip of his fingers.

For a moment it almost seemed that the thick metal walls would resist. Then slowly the vase crumpled inward, until the rose, pinched halfway up its stem, toppled to one side, and water, brimming up over the rim of the vase, ran down onto Paul's contracting hand. Paul relaxed his grasp, opened his hand, and looked down at the squeezed shape of the vase lying in it for a second. Then he tossed the ruin—vase, flower, and all—into the wastebasket by the dresser and flexed his fingers. They were not even cramped. With that much strength the arm should already be becoming muscle-bound and useless. It was not.

He finished dressing and went down to the subway entrance in the basement of the hotel. There was a two-seater among the empty cars waiting on the hotel switchback. He got in and dialed the standard 4441, which was the Directory address in all cities, centers, and Complexes over the fifty-thousand population figure. The little car moved out into the subway traffic and fifteen minutes later deposited him forty miles away at the Directory terminal.

He registered his credit card with Chicago Complex Bookkeeping, and a routing service directed him to a booth on the ninth level. He stepped onto the disk of a large elevator tube along with several other people and found his eye caught by a book a girl was carrying.

The book was in a small, hand-sized portable viewer, and the book's cover looked out at him from the viewer's screen. It gazed at him with the dark glasses and clever old mouth of the face he had been watching that day in the mine. It was the same face. Only, below the chin instead of the formal white collar and knotted scarf, there was the red and gold of some ceremonial robe.

Against this red and gold were stamped the black block letters of the book's title. DESTRUCT.

Glancing up from the book, for the first time he looked at the girl carrying it. She was staring at him with an expression of shock, and at the sight of her face he felt a soundless impact within himself. He found himself

looking directly into the features of the girl who had
stood beside and a little behind the Guildmaster in the
viewing tank of the console at the mine.

"Excuse me," she said. "Excuse me."

She had turned, and pushing blindly past the other
people on the disk stepped quickly off onto the level
above that level on which Paul had entered.

Reflexively, he followed her. But she was already lost
in the crowd. He found himself standing in the heart of
the musical section of the Directory library. He stood,
brushed against by passers-by, gazing vainly out over
the heads of the crowd for the sight of her. He was only
half a pace from a row of booths, and from the partly-
open door of one of these came the thin thread of melody
that was a woman's soprano singing to a chimed ac-
companiment in a slow, minor key. . . .

In apple comfort, long I waited thee

The music ran through him like a wind blowing from
far off, and the pushing people about him became distant and unimportant as shadows. It was the voice of the
girl in the elevator just now. He knew it, though he had
only heard those few words from her. The music swelled
and encompassed him, and one of his moments of feeling moved in on him, on wings too strong for love and
too wide for sadness.

And long I thee in apple comfort waited.

She was the music, and the music was a wind blowing
across an endless snow field to a cavern where ice crystals
chimed to the tendrils of the wind. . . .

In lonely autumn and uncertain springtime
My apple longing for thee was not sated. . . .

Abruptly he wrenched himself free.

Something had been happening to him. He stared about
him, once more conscious of the moving crowd. The
music from the booth was once more only a thread unde

the shuffle of feet and the distant sea-roar of conversations.

He turned around and saw nothing on every side but the prosaic music section of a library floor in the directory. The magic was gone.

But so was the girl.

Paul went on up to the ninth level and found an open booth. He sat down, closed the door, and punched for a list of local psychiatrists, giving his now-registered credit number. As an afterthought, he added a stipulation that the list be restricted to those psychiatrists who had been interested or concerned with the problems of amputees in the past. The board before him flashed an acknowledgment of the request, and a statement that the answer would require about a ten- to fifteen-minute wait.

Paul sat back. On impulse he coded the title of the book the girl had been carrying with a purchase request, and a second later a copy in a commercial viewer was delivered to the desk in front of him from the delivery chute.

He picked it up. The face on the book's cover seemed to be staring at him with a sardonic expression, as if it amused itself with some secret it was keeping from him. The imaged face was not as he had seen it in the viewing tank at the mine, when the features had seemed to refuse to join in a clearly observed face. Now Paul saw the whole face, but something else was wrong. It was not so much a face but a wax mask. Something lifeless and without meaning. Paul punched the trip that would change the cover picture to the first page within.

On the white expanse of paper shown, the title leaped at him once again.

DESTRUCT, by *Walter Blunt*

Paul turned the page. He found himself looking at the first page of an introduction written by someone whose name he did not recognize. Paul skimmed through its half-dozen pages.

Walter Blunt, he read, was the son of rich parents. His

family had owned a controlling interest in one of the great schools of bluefin tuna that followed the circle migratory route between North and South America and Japan. Blunt had grown up brilliant but undisciplined. He had lived the life of the wealthy who have nothing important to do, until one day when with thousands of other hunters he had been caught in an uncontrolled freak early-winter blizzard, while out stalking deer in the Lake Superior Range.

Four others in Blunt's party had died of exposure. Blunt, equally city-bred and unprepared, had in a wry moment conceived of the Alternate Forces of existence, and offered to trade them his life's service for the protection of his life itself. Following this, he had walked unerringly out of the woods to safety and arrived warm and unexhausted at shelter, in spite of the sleeting wind, the dropping temperature, and the fact that he was wearing only the lightest of hunting clothes.

Following this experience, he had dedicated himself to the Alternate Forces. Over a lifetime he had created and organized the Chantry Guild, or Société Chanterie, composed of students of, and graduate workers with, the Alternate Forces. The aim of the Chantry Guild was universal acceptance of the positive principle of destruction. Only by destruction could mankind signify its adherence to the Alternate Laws, and only the Alternate Laws remained strong enough to save mankind from the technical civilization that was now on the verge of trapping mankind like a fly in amber.

The delicate chime of a response counter drew Paul's attention to the screen before him. He looked at a double list of names, addresses, and call numbers. He turned his attention to the typewriter-like keyboard below the screen and tapped out a message to all the names on the list.

My left arm was amputated slightly over seven months ago. My body has to date rejected three attempts to graft on a replacement. No reason for the intolerance can be discovered in the ordinary physiological processes. My physicians have recommended that I explore the possibility of a

*psychological factor being involved in the causes
of the intolerance, and have suggested that I try
my case among psychiatrists of this area, where a
large amount of work with amputees has been done.
Would you be interested in accepting me as a pa-
tient? Paul Allen Formain. File No. 432 36 47865
2551 OG3 K122b, Room 1412, Koh-i-Nor Hotel,
Chicago complex.*

Paul got up, took the book he had just purchased, and
headed back toward the hotel. On the way back and
after he had returned to his room, he read on into Blunt's
writing. Sprawled out on his hotel-room bed he read a
collection of wild nonsense mixed with sober fact, and
an urgent appeal to the reader to enlist himself as a
student under the instruction of some graduate Chantry
Guild member. The reward promised for successfully
completing the course of instruction was apparently to
be a power encompassing all wild dreams of magical
ability that had ever been conceived.

It was too ridiculous to be taken seriously.

Paul frowned.

He found himself holding the book gingerly. It did
not stir in a physical sense, but a vibration came from
it that seemed to quiver deep in the marrow of Paul's
bones. A singing silence began to swell in the room.
One of his moments was coming on him. He held himself still as a wolf come suddenly upon a trap. About
him the walls of the room breathed in and out. The
silence sang louder. The place and moment spoke to
him:

DANGER.

Put the book down.

Louder sang the silence, blinding the ears of his
sensing. . . .

Danger, said the invincible part of him, is a word invented by children, and is essentially meaningless to the
adult.

He pressed the button to turn the page. A new chapter
heading looked up at him.

ALTERNATE FORCES AND REGROWTH. THE RE-

PLACEMENT OF MISSING LIMBS, OR EVEN OF THE
BODY ENTIRE.

*The reparative regeneration of parts of the human
body by epimorphosis, or regrowth beginning
from a regeneration bud or blastema formed at the
wound surface, is a property capable of stimulation
by the Alternate Forces. It has its justification and
instigation in the intended action of self-destruct.
Like all use and manipulation of the Alternate
Forces, the mechanism is simple once the under-
lying principles are grasped. In this case, they are
the Non-Evolutionary (blocking to the Natural
Forces) and the Regressive (actively in reversal of
the Natural Forces). These principles are not
merely statically negative, but dynamically negative,
so that from the fact of their dynamism derives the
energy necessary for the process of regeneration. . . .*

The call note on Paul's room telephone chimed,
breaking the spell. The room fled back to naturalness
and the book sagged in his hand. From the bed he saw
the screen of the phone light up.

"A Directory report on your query, sir," said a
canned voice from the lighted screen.

The screen dissolved into a list of names with medi-
cal and mental science degrees after them. One by one
the names winked out until only one was left. Paul read
it from the bed.

DR. ELIZABETH WILLIAMS

A moment later the word *accept* was printed beside
it. Paul put the book aside where it could be picked
up later.

Chapter 4

". . . How do you feel?"
It was a woman's voice. Paul opened his eyes. Dr

Elizabeth Williams was standing over the chair in which he sat. She put the hypodermic spray gun down on the desk beside him, and walked around to take her seat behind the desk.

"Did I say anything?" Paul sat up straighter in his chair.

"If you mean, did you reply to my questions? no." Dr. Williams looked across the desk at him. She was a small, square-shouldered woman with brown hair and an unremarkable face. "How long have you known about this strong resistance of yours to hypnosis?"

"Is it resistance?" asked Paul. "I'm trying to co-operate."

"How long have you known about it?"

"Since the sailing accident. Five years." Paul looked at her. "What *did* I say?"

Dr. Williams looked at him.

"You told me I was a foolish woman," she said.

Paul blinked at her.

"Is that all?" he asked. "I didn't say anything but that."

"That's all." She looked at him across the desk. He felt curiosity and a sort of loneliness emanating from her. "Paul, can you think of anything in particular that you're afraid of?"

"Afraid?" he asked, and frowned. "Afraid . . . ? Not really. No."

"Worried?"

He thought for a long moment.

"No—not worried, actually," he said. "There's nothing you could say was actually worrying me."

"Unhappy?"

He smiled. Then frowned, suddenly.

"No," he said, and hesitated. "That is, I don't think so."

"Then why did you come to see me?"

He looked at her in some surprise.

"Why, about my arm," he said.

"Not about the fact that you were orphaned at an early age? Not that you've always led a solitary life, with no close friends? Not that you tried to kill your-

self in a sailboat five years ago, and tried again in a
mine, less than a year ago?"

"Wait a minute!" said Paul. She looked at him politely, inquiringly.

"Do you think I arranged those accidents to try and
kill myself?"

"Shouldn't I think so?"

"Why, no," said Paul.

"Why not?"

"Because . . ." A sudden perfect moment of understanding broke through to Paul. He saw her sitting there
in complete blindness. He stared at her, and before his
eyes, looking back at him, she seemed to grow shrunken
and a little older. He got to his feet. "It doesn't matter,"
he said.

"You should think about it, Paul."

"I will. I want to think over this whole business."

"Good," she said. She had not moved out of her
chair, and in spite of the assurance of her tone, she
did not seem quite herself since he had looked at her.
"My receptionist will set up your next time in."

"Thanks," he said. "Good-by."

"Good afternoon, Paul."

He went out. In the outer office the receptionist looked
up from a filing machine as he passed.

"Mr. Formain?" She leaned forward over the machine. "Don't you want to make your next appointment
now?"

"No," said Paul. "I don't think so." He went out.

He went down a number of levels from Dr. Williams'
office to the terminal in the base of the building. There
were public communications booths nearby. He stepped
into one and closed the door. He felt both naked and
relieved. He dialed for a listing of the Chantry Guild
members in the area. The screen lighted up.

Walter Blunt, *Guildmaster* (no listed phone number)

Jason Warren, *Necromancer,* Chantry Guild Secre-
tary, phone number 66 433 35246

Kantele Maki (no listed phone number)

Morton Brown, 66 433 67420
Warra, *Mage*, 64 256 89235
(*The above list contains only the names of those
requesting listing under the Chantry Guild heading.*)

Paul punched 66 433 35246. The screen lighted up
whitely, but it was half a minute before it cleared to
show the face of one of the people Paul remembered
from the television broadcast in the mine a year before,
the face of a thin, black-haired young man with deep-
set, unmoving eyes.

"My name is Paul Formain," said Paul. "I'd like
to talk to Jason Warren."

"I'm Jason Warren. What about?"

"I've just read a book by Walter Blunt that says the
Alternate Forces can grow back limbs that are missing."
Paul moved so that the stub of his left arm was visible
to the other.

"I see." Warren looked at him with the movelessness
of his dark eyes. "What about it?"

"I'd like to talk to you about it."

"I suppose that can be arranged. When would you
like to talk to me?"

"Now," said Paul.

The black eyebrows in the screen went up a fraction.

"Now?"

"I was planning on it," said Paul.

"Oh, you were?"

Paul waited.

"All right, come ahead." Abruptly the screen went
blank, but leaving Paul's vision filled with the after-image
of the dark face that had been in it looking at him with
a curious interest and intent. He rose, breathing out a
little with relief. He had moved without thinking from
the second of perception that had come to him in Elizabeth Williams' office. Suddenly he had realized that her
education and training had made her blind to understanding in his case. She had not understood. That much
ad been explosively obvious. She had been trying to
concile the speed of light with the clumsy mechanism

of the stop watch she believed in. And if she had made
that error, then the psychiatrist at San Diego, after the
boating accident, had been wrong in the same way, as
well.

Paul had reacted without thinking, but, strongly now,
his instinct told him he was right. He had labored under
the handicap of a belief in stop watches. Somewhere,
he told himself now, there was a deeper understanding.
It was a relief to go searching for it at last with an
unfettered mind—a mind awake.

Chapter 5

As Paul entered through the automatically-opening front
door of Jason Warren's apartment, he saw three people
already in the room—a sort of combination office-lounge
—he found himself stepping into.

Two of the three were just going out through a rear
door. Paul got only a glimpse of them—one, a girl who
with a start Paul recognized as the girl with the book
he had encountered earlier at Chicago Directory. The
other was a flat-bodied man in middle age with an air
of quiet competence about him. He, too, had been with
the girl and Blunt on the broadcast Paul had witnessed
in the mine a year before. Paul wondered briefly if
Blunt, also, was nearby. Then the thought passed from
his mind. He found himself looking down, slightly, into
the dark, mercurial face of Jason Warren.

"Paul Formain," said Paul. "I phoned——"

"Sit down." Warren waved Paul into a chair and
took a facing one himself. He looked at Paul with something of the direct, uninhibited stare of a child. "What
can I do for you?"

Paul considered him. Warren sat loosely, almost
sprawled, but with his thin body held in the balance of
a dancer or a highly trained athlete, so that a single
movement might have brought him back to his feet.

"I want to grow a new arm," said Paul.

"Yes," said Warren. He flicked a forefinger toward

phone. "I punched information for your public file after you called," he said. "You're an engineer."

"I was," said Paul, and was a little surprised to hear himself say it, now, with such a small amount of bitterness.

"You believe in the Alternate Laws?"

"No," said Paul. "Truthfully—no."

"But you think they might give you an arm back?"

"It's a chance."

"Yes," said Warren. "An engineer. Hard-headed, practical—doesn't care what makes it work as long as it works."

"Not exactly," said Paul.

"Why bother with the Alternate Laws? Why not just have a new arm out of the culture banks grafted on?"

"I've tried that," said Paul. "It doesn't take."

Warren sat perfectly still for a couple of seconds. There was no change in his face or attitude, but Paul got an impression as if something like a delicately sensitive instrument in the other man had suddenly gone *click* and begun to register.

"Tell me," said Warren, slowly and carefully, "the whole story."

Paul told it. As he talked, Warren sat still and listening. During the fifteen minutes or so it took for Paul to tell it all, the other man did not move or react. And with no warning, even as Paul was talking, it came to Paul where he had seen that same sort of concentration before. It was in a bird dog he had seen once, holding its point, one paw lifted nose straight and tail in line with the body, as still as painted Death.

When Paul stopped, Warren did not speak at once. Instead, without moving a muscle otherwise, he lifted his right hand into the air between them and extended his forefinger toward Paul. The movement had all the remote inevitability of a movement by a machine, or the slow leaning of the top of a chopped tree as it begins its fall.

"Look," Warren said slowly, "at my finger. Look at the tip of my finger. Look closely. Right there at the end of the nail, under the nail, you can see a spot of red. 't's a drop of blood coming out from under the nail.

See it swelling there. It's getting larger. In a moment it'll drop off. But it's getting larger, larger——"

"No," said Paul. "There's no drop of blood there at all. You're wasting your time—and mine."

Warren dropped his hand.

"Interesting," he said. "Interesting."

"Is it?" asked Paul.

"Graduate members of the Chantry Guild," said Warren, "can't be hypnotized, either. But you say you don't believe in the Alternate Laws."

"I seem to be a sort of free-lance, then," said Paul.

Warren rose suddenly from his chair with the single motion Paul had expected. He walked lightly and easily across the room, turned, and came back.

"In order to resist hypnosis," he said, standing over Paul, "you must make use of the Alternate Laws, whether you recognize them as such or not. The keystone of the use of the Alternate Laws is complete independence of the individual—independence from any force, physical or otherwise."

"And vice versa?" asked Paul, smiling.

"And vice versa." Warren did not smile. He stood looking down at Paul. "I'll ask you again," he said. "What do you expect me to do for you?"

"I want an arm," said Paul.

"I can't give you an arm," said Warren. "I can't do anything for you. The use of the Alternate Laws is for those who would do things for themselves."

"Show me how, then."

Warren sighed slightly. It was a sigh that sounded to Paul not only weary, but a little angry.

"You don't know what the hell you're asking," said Warren. "To train whatever aptitude you have for use of the Alternate Laws, I'd have to take you on as my apprentice in necromancy."

"Blunt's book gave me to understand the Guild was eager for people."

"Why, we are," said Warren. "We have an urgent need right now for someone comparable to Leonardo da Vinci. We'd be very glad to get someone with the qualifications of Milton or Einstein. Of course, what we really need i

someone with a talent no one has conceived of yet—
a sort of X-Genius. So we advertise."

"Then you don't want people."

"I didn't say that," said Warren. He turned and paced
the room and came back. "You're serious about joining
the Guild?"

"If it'll get me my arm."

"It won't get you your arm. I tell you, no one can
put that arm back but you. There's a relation between
the Alternate Laws and the work of the Guild, but it
isn't what you think."

"Perhaps I'd better be enlightened," said Paul.

"All right," said Warren. He put his hands in his pockets
and stood with shoulders hunched slightly, looking down
at Paul. "Try this on for size. This is an ill world we
live in, Formain. A world sick from a surfeit of too many
technical luxuries. An overburdened world, swarming with
people close to the end of their ropes." His deep-set eyes
were steady on Paul. "People today are like a man
who thought that if he made his success in the world,
everything else that makes life good would come automatically. Now they've made their success—the perfection
of a technological civilization in which no one lacks anything in the way of a physical comfort—and they find
themselves in a false paradise. Like an electric motor
without a load upon it, the human spirit without the
weight of the need to achieve and progress is beginning to
rev up toward dissolution. Faster and faster, until they'll
fly apart and destroy this world they've made."

He stopped.

"What do you say to that?" he asked.

"It might be the case," said Paul. "I don't really believe that's the situation we're in, myself, but it might
be the case."

"All right," said Warren. "Now try this: In a climate
of confusion, one of the surest ways of confounding the
enemy is to tell him the plain truth. And the Guildmaster has stated the plain truth plainly in his book. The
Chantry Guild is not interested in propagating the use of
the Alternate Laws. It only wants to train and make use
of those who can already use the Laws, to its own end.
And that end's to hurry the end that is inevitably com-

ing, to bring about the destruction of present civilization."

Warren stopped. He seemed to wait for Paul to say something. But Paul also waited.

"We," said Warren, "are a small but powerful revolutionary body with the aim of driving this sick world into complete insanity and collapse. The Alternate Laws are real, but most of our structure is completely fake. If you come in as my apprentice, you'll be committed to the job of destroying the world."

"And that's my only way to a use of the Alternate Forces?" asked Paul.

"For you to accept the Guild's philosophy and aim, yes," said Warren. "Otherwise, no."

"I don't believe that," said Paul. "If your Alternate Forces exist, they'll work for me as well as all the Chantry Guild put together."

Warren dropped into a chair and stared at Paul for a long moment.

"Arrogant," he said. "Completely arrogant. Let's see. . . ." He rose lightly to his feet, crossed the room, and touched a spot on one of the walls.

The wall slid back, revealing an area which seemed half modern laboratory and half alchemist's den. On the table in its center were earthenware containers, some metal jars, and a large flask full of dark-red liquid.

Warren opened a drawer in the table, and took out something which his body hid from Paul's view. He closed the drawer, turned, and came back carrying a rather decrepit-looking conch shell, brown-stained and polished by handling and age.

He put the shell down on an occasional table a few feet from Paul's chair.

"What does that do?" Paul asked, looking at it curiously.

"For me," said Warren, "it does a lot of things. Which is no advantage to you except that we might say it's been sensitized to the action of the Alternate Laws. Let's see if this arrogance of yours can do anything with it."

Paul frowned. He stared at the shell. For a second th[e] situation was merely ridiculous. And then it was as if [a] thread of brightness ran through him. There was a su[dden]

den weird sensation, as if a great, deep gong sounded, somewhere deep inside him. And then a rushing, back in the depths of his mind, as if a host of memories long forgotten ran and beat upon a locked door held shut to them since he could not exactly remember when.

The conch shell stirred. It rolled to a point of balance and hung there. The bright daylight lanced through a far window of the room and a faint wisp of some light music sounded from the apartment next door. A thin, reedy voice spoke faintly but clearly from the shell.

"From greater dark into the little light. And then once more to greater dark he goes."

The beating on the locked door in Paul's mind dwindled away into silence. The shell lost its balance and fell over, still, on one side. Across from Paul, Warren drew a deep breath and picked up the shell.

"You may be a natural," he said.

"A natural?" Paul looked up at him.

"There are certain abilities in the province of the Alternate Powers which can be possessed by those who know nothing of the true nature of the Alternate Powers. Mind reading, for example. Or artistic inspiration."

"Oh?" said Paul. "How do you tell the difference between people with that, and your Alternate Power people?"

"Very simply," answered Warren. But the tone of his voice and the way he held the shell and continued to watch Paul did not imply simpleness. "For such people their abilities work spasmodically and unreliably. For us, they always work."

"For example, mind reading?"

"I'm a Necromancer," said Warren, shortly, "not a seer. Besides, I used the common, recognizable term. I'm told minds aren't so much *read* as experienced."

"When you go into someone else's mind, you lose your own point of view?"

"Yes," said Warren, "you must be a natural." He took the conch shell back across to the cabinet and put it away. He turned around and spoke from where he was.

"You've got something," he said. "It may be a valuable attitude, and it may not. But I'm willing to take you on a probationary apprentice. If I think you have promise after a while, you'll be taken fully into the Guild on an apprenticeship basis. If that happens, you'll be required to assign everything you own and all future personal income to the Guild. But if it reaches that point, you needn't worry about material things." Warren's lips twisted slightly. "The Guild will take care of you. Study and learn, and you'll be able to grow your arm back one day."

Paul stood up.

"You guarantee me an arm?" he said.

"Of course," said Warren. He did not move from where he stood, watching Paul across the widths of laboratory and apartment room with unmoving gaze.

Chapter 6

Shuttling through the many-leveled maze of the Chicago Complex's streets and buildings in a one-man subway car, Paul leaned his head back against the cushions of the seat and closed his eyes.

He was exhausted, and exhaustion, he now suspected, had its roots in something besides the physical efforts he had been put to today. Something almost physical had taken place in him following his recognition of the ridiculousness of the psychiatric approach to his situation. And the business with the shell had also drained him.

But the exhaustion was something that rest could cure. More important were two other things. The first of these was a clear recognition that too many things were happening around him and to him for them all to be accidents. And accidents, once the notion that he was subconsciously bent on self-destruction had been discarded, had been the obvious alternative answer.

The second was the fact that the Necromancer, Warren, had called him arrogant.

Disturbed by this, Paul for the first time faced the fact that such disturbance was unusual with him. Now that he stopped to consider the fact, in spite of all that had hpened to him it had never before occurred to him that he might be at the mercy of any other force than that of his own will. Perhaps, he thought, this was arrogance, but the idea did not ring true. Above all else, he trusted his own feelings, and he did not feel arrogant. All that came to him when he reached back into himself for reasons was a calm feeling of certainty. It was that invincible element in him which took all things calmly.

For, thought Paul, leaning back with his eyes closed, above all he must not be arrogant. He was like a man peering through the glass-clearness of still water into the secret life of a tide pool on an ocean beach. Wonderful things were happening just a little before him, and would continue to happen as long as the pool was not disturbed. But a touch of wind or a dabbled finger, a ripple across the water's surface, and the life going on under his nose would no longer be isolated, pure, and complete. Gentleness was the watchword. Gentleness and extreme care. Already he had begun to separate and identify elements: by a hint of movement, a change of color, an emerging shape. . . .

Leaning back with his eyes closed, Paul lost himself in a half-doze and a dream of things half-seen.

Sudden deceleration of his small car pulled him upright in his seat. The car jerked to a stop. He opened his eyes and looked out through the unopaqued bubble of the car's top.

He was at a mid-level intersection of streets. Above and below him were residential and business layers of the great three-dimensional community that was Chicago Complex. On his own level his car had halted part-way out into an intersection the four corners of which were occupied by small shops and offices, beyond which was a large recreation area, parklike with trees. But no people were visible. The shops were empty. The park was empty. The streets were clear and still.

Paul once more leaned forward and pressed for the terminal at the Koh-i-Nor Hotel. The car did not move. He punched for the transportation control center, malfunction division.

The communications tank above the car's dashboard lighted up.

"Sir?" said a woman's canned voice. "Can I help you?"

"I'm in a one-man car that won't move," said Paul. "It's stopped at the intersection of—" he glanced at a street-corner sign—"N Level 2432 and AANB."

"Checking," said the canned voice. There was a moment's wait and the voice spoke again. "Sir? Are you certain of your location. The area you report yourself in has been closed to traffic. Your car could not have entered it in the last half hour."

"It seems to have anyway." Paul broke off suddenly. He seemed to have heard something odd. He got out of the car and stood up alongside. it. The sound came thinly but more clearly to his ears. It was the noise of people chanting, and the noise was approaching.

"The area you report yourself in," the tank in the car was saying, "has been cleared to allow for a public demonstration. Would you please check your location again? If it is the location you have already reported, please leave your car at once and ascend one level immediately to find another. Repeat, leave your car *immediately*."

Paul swung away from the car. Across the street from him was an escalator spiral ramp. He reached it and let himself be borne upward. It swung up and out over the street he had just left. The chanting now came clearly to his ears. It was not words, but sounds without meaning.

"Hey, hey! Hey, hey! Hey, hey! . . ."

Puzzled, he stepped off the upward-moving surface of the ramp and looked out over the chest-high siding. Down around a curve of the cross street to the one on which his car had stalled he saw people pouring toward him in a sort of orderly mob, twenty abreast, and filling the street solidly from curb to curb.

They came quickly. They were at jog trot. Young men and women for the most part wearing blue slacks, white shirts, and green-colored, odd, cocked hats. They ran with arms interlinked, in step with the rhythm of their chanting.

Abruptly, Paul identified them. They represented, evidently, one of the so-called marching societies. Such groups gathered together for no other purpose than to run through the streets perhaps once or twice a month

It was a sort of controlled and channeled hysteria, or so Paul remembered reading. Such exercises blew off a lot of emotional steam safely, said the societies' advocates. For unless the group ran directly into some obstacle, they did no harm and were not harmed.

They came on now and Paul could see their eyes, which were all fixed straight ahead. But their gazes were not glassy, as of people drunk or drugged. Rather, they were clear, but fixed, as with people undergoing a moment of exaltation or frenzy. They were almost below Paul, now. Almost to the intersection.

Suddenly, Paul realized that his one-man car, stalled where it was, would be in their way. They were practically upon it now. The cadenced slapping of their river of feet was shaking the ramp on which he stood. It was making, it seemed, the whole structure of the city Complex, level on level, vibrate to a high, almost supersonic singing. A wave of heat struck up to them from their on-rushing bodies, and the louder, ever-louder yelping of their chant rocked on his ears like the unnatural amplification of sounds heard in a fever. Whirlpooled about by noise and heat, Paul saw their first ranks run into his empty car and, without halting, like a stampede of mindless cattle, tumble it, rolling, over and over until it bounced at last to a railing overhanging the level below. Paul watched it mount the railing and drop from sight, the ultimate noise of its impact below lost in the encompassing noise of the running crowd.

He looked back along the road, in the direction from which they had come. The river of people was unended, still passing out of sight around the curve. But now, as he watched, the final ranks began to thin and quieten, and over the other sounds he heard the thin wail of ambulance sirens following slowly after.

Paul went on up to the level above, found a two-man car that was empty on a siding, and returned to the hotel.

When he got to his room, the door was open. A small, gray man in a business suit rose smoothly from a chair as Paul entered, and offered an opened wallet cardcase for Paul's inspection.

"Hotel security, Mr. Formain," said the small man. "My name's James Butler."

"Yes?" said Paul. He felt his tiredness like a cloak around him.

"A routine matter, Mr. Formain. Maintenance discovered a vase in your room that had been rather bent out of shape."

"Put it on my bill," said Paul. "Now, if you don't mind——"

"The vase isn't important, Mr. Formain. But we understand you have been seeing a psychiatrist?"

"A Dr. Elizabeth Williams. Today. Why?"

"As a routine matter, this hotel asks for and is notified if any of its guests are currently under psychiatric care. The Chicago Complex Public Health Unit permits us to refuse occupancy to guests who might disturb the hotel. Of course, no such refusal is anticipated in your case, Mr. Formain."

"I'm checking out in the morning," said Paul.

"Oh? I'm sorry to hear that," said James Butler evenly. "I assure you there was no intention to offend you. It's just one of the management rules that we inform our guests that we have been notified about them."

"I was leaving anyway," said Paul. He looked at the man's unchanging face and motionless body, and James Butler's personality came clearly through to him. Butler was a dangerous little man. An efficient little machine of suspicion and control. Underneath, though, was something repressed, something guarded by an inner fear. "Right now, I want to turn in. So if you don't mind . . ."

Butler inclined his head slightly.

"Unless, of course," he said, "there's something more."

"Nothing."

"Thank you." Butler turned and walked smoothly to the door. "Feel free to call on hotel services at any time," he said, and went out, closing the door behind him.

Paul frowned. But weariness was like a great load on him. He undressed and dropped into the bed. And sleep closed down about him like great, gray wings, enfoldin

He dreamed that he walked a cobbled road, in da ness under the stars, alone. And the cobbles grew as went until they were great boulders to be climbed. And then that dream vanished and he dreamed that he was paralyzed, drifting upright through the nighttime streets of the Chicago Complex. He drifted along without touching the ground and after a while he came on an arc light on its pole that had been changed into a monstrous candy cane. And just beyond it a store front had been turned from plastic to ice, and was melting.

In the morning he woke feeling as if he had slept fourteen years, rather than fourteen hours, packed, and went down to the main lobby to pay his bill.

He cut through one of the hotel bars on his way down to the basement terminal. At this early hour it was all but deserted except for a plump middle-aged man who sat alone at a table with a small tulip-shaped glass of some purplish liquid before him. For a moment, passing, Paul thought that the man was drunk. And then he caught the scent of cinnamon from the glass and saw the man's eyes had pinpoint pupils. And looking beyond this, he caught sight of Butler, seated in the darkness of a corner, watching. Paul went over to the hotel security man.

"Are you notified about drug addicts, too?" Paul asked.

"Our bars stock the non-habit-forming synthetics," said Butler. "It's quite legal."

"You didn't answer my question," said Paul.

"The hotel," said Butler, "feels a certain responsibility to certain guests." He glanced up at Paul. "That's legal, too. And any extra charges are quite reasonable. If you hadn't already planned to leave, Mr. Formain, I could have told you what services we had available."

Paul turned and went on. He found a one-man car at the terminal, and, getting in, punched for Warren's apartment. The first demand the Necromancer had made of his probationary apprentice was that Paul should move into the apartment, where Warren could have him under constant observation.

He found Warren waiting for him. The Necromancer turned over one of the bedrooms in the apartment to him, and then to all intents and purposes left Paul to his own devices. For the rest of the week Paul hardly saw he intense young man.

It was five days later that Paul, thoroughly bored with the apartment by this time, happened to be going through the music Warren had listed in his apartment player. Abruptly, he came across a title which caught his attention.

IN APPLE COMFORT . . . vocal. Sung by *Kantele*

Kantele. Suddenly the mental connection was made. It had been there in the list of local members of the Chantry Guild. *Kantele Maki.* And he remembered now, there was a girl who sang professionally under the single name *Kantele.* She was the girl with the book that he had first seen on the news broadcast, and after that at the Directory. He pressed the small black button alongside the initial letter of the song title.

There was the barest second of a pause, and then the chimed music rose softly ringing from the player, interspersed by the cool, shifting silver of the voice he recognized.

> *In apple comfort, long I waited thee*
> *And long I thee in apple comfort waited.*
> *In lonely autumn and uncertain——*

A sudden gasp from behind him made Paul shut off the player abruptly and turn about. He found himself facing the girl herself.

She stood a little to one side of a bookcase of old-fashioned volumes. But the bookcase, to Paul's surprise, was swung out from its usual place, revealing not a wall behind it, but an entrance to a small room furnished and equipped like an office. Seeing his gaze go to it, Kantele broke suddenly out of the rigidity that had been holding her, and, putting out a hand, pushed the bookcase back into position, closing the entrance. They stood, looking across the room at each other.

"I didn't know . . ." she said. "I forgot you were living here now."

He watched her, curiously. She was noticeably pale.

"Did you think I was someone else?" he asked.

"Yes. I mean"—she said—"I thought you were Jas

She was one of the kind who lie defiantly. He felt her untruthfulness across all the distance separating them.

"You've got a fine voice," he said. "I was playing that song of yours——"

"Yes. I heard you," she interrupted. "I—I'd rather you wouldn't play it, if you don't mind."

"Would you?" asked Paul.

"It has associations for me. If you don't mind . . ."

"I won't play it if you don't want me to, of course," said Paul. He walked toward her and then stopped suddenly, seeing her reflexively take the one step back from him that the wall behind her allowed.

"Jase . . ." she said. "Jase will be here at any minute."

Paul watched her, frowning a bit. He felt puzzled and a little exasperated by her, but also oddly touched, as he might be by anyone or anything defenseless that did not realize he meant it no harm. And that was odd too, because Kantele did not give the impression generally of defenselessness, but of wire-like courage. Paul was reaching to approach this problem in words when the sound of the opening front door of the apartment brought both their heads around in its direction.

Warren and the flat-bodied, crop-haired man Paul had seen in the news broadcast, and again leaving the apartment with Kantele the first time he had come to see Warren, had just come in. They headed straight for Paul and Kantele.

Chapter 7

"You didn't answer the door," said Warren, stopping before them and looking at Kantele.

"You didn't ring," said Paul.

"He means me—my apartment, next door," said Kantele, but without looking away from Warren to Paul. "I forgot he was here, Jase. I heard noise and I knew you were out. I stepped in from the office."

"Yes," said Warren. His thin, dark, bright face looked from her to Paul without smiling. "Well, you'd have met

anyway. You know each other now? This is Paul Formain, Kantele. Paul, Kantele Maki."

"How do you do?" said Paul to her, and smiled. She
gave a little spasm of a smile back.

"And this is Burton McLeod."

"McCloud?" echoed Paul, shaking hands with the flat-
bodied man.

"Spelled McLeod, pronounced McCloud," said McLeod.
His voice was mild and a little husky. His handgrip was
dry and firm. His brown eyes were the lonely, sad, and
savage eyes of a hawk on leash and perch. A week before,
the hotel security man, Butler, had impressed Paul as
dangerous. McLeod radiated dangerousness of a different
order. If Butler was like a stiletto, needle-pointed and
polished, then this man was scarred and heavy as some
ancient broadsword.

While Paul and McLeod had been shaking hands, Warren and Kantele had held each other's eyes for a long
second. Now, suddenly, Warren turned away from her
with a quickness that was almost like a shrug and took a
small box from his pocket. He opened it in front of Paul.

Paul saw neat rows of white gelatine capsules within.
Warren took one out and handing the box aside to Mc-
Leod, broke it and poured a white powder from it into
his palm.

"Taste," said Warren. Paul frowned.

"It's quite harmless," said Warren. He dipped a finger in
the powder himself, and put it to his tongue. Paul hesitated a second and then followed suit. He tasted sweet-
ness.

"Sugar?" said Paul, looking at Warren.

"That's right." The Necromancer dusted off his hands
over a nearby ash tray. "But to the man you'll be giving
it to it'll be cocaine. I said"—Warren stared at Paul
tightly—"it'll *be* cocaine. The minute you let the box into
anyone's hands but your own. I mention this so that
you'll realize you're legally in the clear in delivering it, as
long as you keep it in your pocket until the last moment."

"You want me to deliver it?" asked Paul. "Who to?"

"You know how the Koh-i-Nor's laid out. I want you
to take this box to suite 2309. Don't ask directions from
the desk clerk or anyone else. Give it to the man you

find there. If you run into any trouble . . ." Warren hesitated and glanced for a second at Kantele. "I don't expect you will. But if you do, there's a chess tournament going on on the sixtieth level in the banquet rooms there. Go up there and look for Kantele. She'll get you out."

He stopped talking. There was a moment of silence in the room.

"If it was cocaine," said Paul, "of course I wouldn't take it."

"You'll be carrying sugar," said Warren. His thin face seemed to flash for a second like a drawn blade in the brightness of the sunlight coming through the far windows of the room. "It'll be transmuted into the drug only after you deliver it. You can believe or not believe, go or part company with me, just as you like."

"I'll take it," said Paul. He held out his hand. McLeod gave him the box. "Twenty-three-o-nine?"

"Twenty-three-o-nine," said Warren. The eyes of all three followed him, Paul could feel in the muscles of his back, as he took the box and left the apartment.

The desk clerk he passed at the Koh-i-Nor was a stranger and did not look up as Paul went by. Paul took the elevator tube to the twenty-seventh level.

It turned out to be a level of modern-décor, semi-VIP suites. The type of establishments that would require income in excess of forty thousand a year to be supported without strain by their occupants. Paul walked down the wide, tiled hallway, coolly lighted by the high, blue-curtained windows at each end of it, until he came to a door marked with the numerals 2309. Below it in small letters were the two words *service entrance*.

Paul touched the door. It was not only unlocked but ajar. It swung noiselessly back into its wall recess at his touch. He stepped into the kitchen of the suite.

Voices broke on his ear from elsewhere in the suite. He stopped dead, and with a faint noise the door slid closed again behind him. One of the voices was an incisive, middle-aged tenor, sharp with emotion. The other was thick and deeper in tone, stumbling, sullen.

". . . pull yourself together!" the tenor voice was saying. The deeper voice muttered something unintelligible.

"You know better than that!" said the tenor. "You don't want to be cured, that's what it is. The substitutes were bad enough. But your monkeying around with real drugs makes you a danger to the whole Department, if not the whole Division. Why didn't you take psychiatric leave when I offered it to you last March?"

The heavy voice muttered something, it seemed to Paul, about the soup, or super.

"Get that out of your head!" said the tenor. "You've let the statistics on mental health get you to seeing ghosts in the woodwork. Electronic equipment is electronic equipment. No more. No less. Don't you think that if there was anything more there, *I*'d know it?"

"Unless . . ." muttered the heavy voice, "got you already."

"For your own sake"—the tenor was disgusted—"see your physician. Get yourself committed. I won't investigate your Department for the next four days. That'll give you time to get safely into a hospital room where you can decently refuse to answer questions. That's it, now. It's up to you." There was the sound of footsteps walking across hard flooring and a door button snapped to unlatch. "Four days. I won't give you an hour more."

A wind of sudden suspicion blew coolly through Paul, chilling him. He turned quickly himself, stepped silently back through the door he had just entered, and out into the hall. There was a small alcove in the wall about six feet to his left. He stepped to it and pressed himself, back to its wall, deep in its shadow, looking along the hall to 2309's main entrance.

It opened immediately. A small, sparely erect man with thin gray hair came out, closed the door behind him, and went away from Paul toward the far set of elevator tubes at the other end of the hall. For a second as he turned to the elevators, Paul saw a sparrow-like profile against the blue illumination from the curtain windows, and recognized the man. In the suite the tenor voice had sounded vaguely familiar, and Paul had thought it might be the security man, Butler, speaking. But he saw now that there was another reason he had half-recognized the voice.

The man by the elevators was Kirk Tyne, World Com

plex Engineer. He was the executive head of the theoretical machinery that correlated the activities of the interlocking Complexes of technological devices that made modern life possible about the planet. In theory he and his Division of Engineers performed the functions of a sort of super-computing element, since sooner or later mechanical decisions had to find their ultimate authority and review in human ones. He reached out his hand now to open the elevator tube.

He had not quite touched it when a fair portion of the blue illumination from the window was suddenly occulted by the dark, wide-shouldered body of a tall man who stepped off the downshaft alongside the one toward which Tyne was reaching.

"Well, Kirk," said the tall man. "Didn't expect to see you here."

His voice struck and reverberated on Paul's listening ear like the little echoes chasing each other, on and on, from the sound of a gong struck in some deep and stony cave. It was the voice of Walter Blunt. Almost involuntarily, Paul stepped forward to the edge of his recess to get a better look at this head of the Chantry Guild. But Blunt was standing just so slightly turned that his face was shadowed and averted from Paul.

"Got off here by mistake," replied Tyne, sharply and smoothly. "I was headed for the chess matches upstairs. How about you, Walt?"

"Why," Blunt leaned on his heavy cane, and his voice had a humorous note in it, "I saw you and stepped out to say hello. Headed for the lobby myself for a moment, to meet someone. You look good, Kirk." He laid aside his cane, leaning it against the wall of a tube, and offered his hand. Tyne shook it.

"Thank you, Walter," said Tyne, shaking hands. He added, drily, "I imagine we'll both live a while, yet."

"Why, no, Kirk," said Blunt. "The instrument of Armageddon is already at work. I intend to survive the conflict when it comes, but I don't expect you will."

Tyne shook his head.

"You amaze me, Walt," he said. "You know very well I'm the one man who knows all about your little sect—right down to the fact that it numbers only a little more than sixty thousand members, scattered all over the globe. Yet you keep on insisting to my face that you're about to take over the world. And what would you do with it, once you'd taken it over? You can't run things without the very Complex technologies you claim you intend to destroy."

"Well, now," said Blunt, "there're a lot of different versions of this world of ours, Kirk. You've got one, with your Complexes of equipment—a nice steady-ticking world. The only pity is, it won't stop growing and complicating itself. Then, there's the world of the fanatics, the people who go in for dangerous sports, wild cults, and marching societies. And then again, there's the vague, gauzy world of the spiritually inclined, and the world of the asymbolic pioneers, artist and scientist. There's the world of those to whom tradition and an anchored existence are the only worthwhile basis for life. There's even the world of the psychotics, the neurotically crippled."

"You talk," said Tyne, "as if these other . . . attitudes, had an equal value with normal civilized society."

"But they have, Kirk, they have," said Blunt, looming over the smaller man. "Ask anyone who belongs to one of them. Don't look at me, man. This is your world—the world you boys made out of the industrial revolution three hundred years ago. To put it somewhat crudely, if this here's heaven, how come we still got stomach-aches?"

"We got stomach-aches," said Tyne, stepping a little aside toward his elevator tubes. "But we also got doctors to physic 'em. Which we didn't always have before. If you'll excuse me, Walt, I want to get upstairs to the chess matches. Are you coming back up?"

"Right away," said Blunt. Tyne stepped onto a disk floating up the tube beside him, with one foot. The disk checked itself. "And how's Mrs. Tyne been?" asked Blunt.

"Excellent," said Tyne. He stepped completely onto the disk and was borne upward out of sight.

Blunt turned, stepped through the open door of the down tube onto a descending disk, and disappeared himself.

Paul came out from the shadow, still looking toward the elevators where the two men had stood. They were gon now, but Blunt's stick was still leaning where he had placed it before shaking hands with Tyne. Paul remembered abruptly how Blunt had stood, half-turned away from the alcove. It came to Paul that he had never got a square look at the head of the Chantry Guild. Before, this had been only a minor omission in the back of his mind. But suddenly it moved to the forefront.

Paul was suddenly conscious of something that most of the time he merely took for granted. That for him to meet someone was automatically to gain a great deal of insight into them. And Blunt was an enigma. But an enigma with whom Paul's life had become considerably entangled. With Blunt, as with the Guild itself, there seemed to be considerably more going on than met the eye. Deciding, Paul strode out from his alcove, down to the elevators, and picked up the stick. Blunt could hardly avoid facing the man who returned his walking stick to him in person.

Paul came back to suite 2309, the main entrance this time, the one through which he had seen Tyne leave. He pressed the door button. It was unlocked and opened at his touch. He stepped inside, closing the door behind him, and found himself in the sitting room of the suite, and facing the man he had seen drugged and under watch by Butler in the hotel bar, the morning of his leaving.

The sound of the closing door brought the man's head around. He had been half-turned away, blowing his nose on a tissue. At the click of the door's latching, he jerked about to face Paul. And then he went backward across the room, mouthing and stumbling like a creature scared out of all common, ordinary sense, until the high, wide window of the room stopped him.

He stood, trapped and staring, blinking, shivering, pushing against the window as if he could shove himself through it into the twenty-three levels of unblocked air that separated him from the ground level before the hotel.

Paul checked instinctively. And the wave of sick fear emanating from the man crested and broke over Paul like solid ocean surf. Paul stood, momentarily and in spite of himself, stunned. He had never thought a thinking being could go so bad.

The man's eyes flicked and bored into Paul. The

eyes themselves were watering, and the nose sniffled un-
controllably. The man's face was gray and rigid. Something mangled whimpered within him.

"It's all right," said Paul. "All right . . ." He came gently
toward the man, Blunt's stick tucked under his right arm
and the box of capsules in his single hand outstretched.
"Here . . . I'm just bringing you these. . . ."

The man continued to stare and sniffle spasmodically.
Paul, now within arm's length of him, laid the box down
on a table. As an afterthought, he opened it with two
fingers and took out one of the white capsules.

"See?" he said. "Here . . ." He held it out to the man,
but the other, either jerkily reaching for it, or jerkily
pushing it away, knocked it from Paul's fingers. Automatically, Paul bent to pick it up.

His head was still down when warning rang loud within
him. He straightened up suddenly to see the drug addict
facing him now, a small handgun black and deadly in one
trembling hand. The pinhole of its muzzle wavered at
Paul's chest.

"Easy," said Paul. "Easy . . ."

His voice seemed not even to reach the ears of the
other man. The drug addict stepped forward and Paul
automatically stepped back.

"It sent you," said the man, hoarsely. "It sent you."

"Nothing sent me," said Paul. "I came to bring you
that box on the table. There it is." He nodded toward it.

The man did not look at it. Moving out into the room,
he began to circle Paul, while keeping gun and eyes aimed
at Paul.

"I'm going to kill you," he said. "You think I won't
kill you, but I will."

"Why?" asked Paul. And that monosyllable, he thought,
should at least have made the other pause, but again it
seemed the drug addict did not even hear him.

"It sent you to kill me," said the man. "It can't kill.
It isn't built to allow itself to kill. But it can fix things
so some other factor does the dirty work."

"I don't want to hurt you," said Paul.

"It's no use," said the man. Paul could sense the will
to pull the trigger accumulating in the mind opposite
him. The man's back began to straighten with somethin

like pride. "I understand, you see. I know all about it."

The man was almost between Paul and the room's entrance, now. He was at a distance of about eight feet, out of arm's reach. Paul made a move to step toward him and the tiny muzzle of the gun came up sharply.

"No, no!" said the man. *"No!"*

Paul stopped. He became conscious suddenly of the hard roundness of Blunt's walking stick under his arm. It was a good three feet in length. Paul began to let the stick slip down into his hand.

"Just a little," said the man. "Just a moment more . . . It thought you'd find me alone here. It didn't know I had a gun. When you steal something, there's no way for it to know. No record—*what're you doing?"*

The last three words came out in a scream, as the man noticed the end of the walking stick slide into Paul's hand. The pinhole muzzle leaped up and forward. Paul jumped aside and forward. There was no time to throw the stick as he had planned. He saw the man swinging to bring the gun's aim upon him. The other was close.

"Now!" screamed the man. The walking stick leaped in Paul's grasp and he felt it connect solidly. The man fell away from him.

The man fell and rolled over on his back on the carpet. The small gun tumbled foolishly out of his hand. He lay, looking in terrified accusation at the ceiling.

Still holding the walking stick, Paul stepped forward. He stared down at the drug addict. The man lay still. His bloodshot eyes did not focus upon Paul. Paul lifted the stick in his hand and stared at it. The dark wood was dented and splintered a little but in no way broken or weakened. Paul looked back down at the man on the floor, letting the heavy weight of his unnaturally muscled right arm, holding the stick, drop limply at his side.

Among the sparse black hair on the man's skull, the blood was beginning to flow, slowly and darkly. Paul felt emptiness inside him, as if he had deeply inhaled on nothingness. The broken skull looked as if it had been stricken almost in two by some heavy sword.

Chapter 8

The man's dead, thought Paul. He took a deep, shuddering breath, but the emptiness inside him did not go away. *Why don't I feel anything more than this?*

Once he would have expected an answer from the unconquerable element back in the depths of his mind. But with the overgrowth of his right arm, and the decision in the psychiatrist's office, that part of him seemed to have melted into the rest of his consciousness. He was all of one piece now. Still, he could almost imagine he heard the ghost of a whisper replying to his thought.

Death, it whispered, *is a factor also.*

The stick was still poised in his hand. Paul opened his hand about it and a small object fell onto the carpet. He bent and picked it up. It was the capsule he had offered the dead man, flattened and bent now from being between his palm and the walking stick. He put it in his pocket. Swiftly he turned and went out of the suite.

He closed the door behind him and was halfway to the same elevator tubes which Tyne and Blunt had taken, when his mind started working sensibly again. He stopped dead.

Why should he run, he asked himself? He had only acted in self-defense on being attacked by what amounted to an insane man waving a gun. Paul went back into 2309 and used the phone there to call the hotel's security office.

The office answered without lighting up the vision tank. A voice spoke to him from out of blank grayness.

"Who is calling, please?"

"Suite 2309. But I'm not a guest of the hotel. I want to report——"

"One minute, please."

There was a moment of silence. The tank still did not light up. Then suddenly it cleared and Paul found himself looking into the neat, expressionless features of James Butler.

"Mr. Formain," said Butler. "I was informed twenty-eight minutes ago that you had entered the hotel by the plaza entrance."

"I was bringing something——"

"So we assumed," said Butler. "As a matter of routine, our hall monitor cameras are lighted to follow nonguests under conditions when we haven't been notified of their visit in advance. Is the occupant of suite 2309 with you now, Mr. Formain?"

"Yes," said Paul. "But I'm afraid there's been an accident here."

"Accident?" Butler's voice and expression stayed invariable.

"The man I met here threatened me with a gun." Paul hesitated. "He's dead."

"Dead?" asked Butler. For a second he merely looked at Paul. "You must be mistaken about the gun, Mr. Formain. We have a complete file and check on the occupant of 2309. He did not own a gun."

"No. He told me he stole it."

"I don't mean to argue with you, Mr. Formain. But I must inform you that in accordance with police regulations this conversation is being irreversibly recorded."

"Recorded!" Paul stared into the tank.

"Yes, Mr. Formain. You see, we happen to know that it would have been impossible for the resident in 2309 to steal any kind of weapon. He has been under constant surveillance by our staff."

"Well, your staff slipped up!"

"I'm afraid that's impossible, too. The only way a gun could have entered the suite where you are now would have been if you had carried it in yourself."

"Just a minute." Paul leaned down toward the tank. "Mr. Kirk Tyne, the World Complex Engineer, was here just before I came."

"Mr. Tyne," said Butler, "left the North Tower lobby at 14:09 by up tube on the elevators and arrived at the chess tournament on the sixtieth level at 14:10. Our hall monitors show no one entering 2309 in the past six hours but you. Accordingly . . ."

The barest flicker of Butler's eyes to the side woke Paul suddenly to the nearness of the trap into which he was sliding. The hotel security agent was no mean hypnotist himself. The dead monotony of his voice, the expressionless face that classed all things with the dull unimportance of a lost hotel key or misdirected luggage, would have been lethal against anyone who lacked Paul's inherent immunity.

Without waiting even to shut off the phone Paul moved, letting his reflexes take over. He was at the door and through it into the hall before Butler had time to stop talking. The hall outside was empty.

Moving swiftly, Paul turned from the elevators and raced down the hall to a heavy fire door. He pulled it open and passed through into the concrete shaft of a stairway. He found himself on a small landing with steps leading up from one end and down from another. The edge of another fire door recessed in its slot in the wall stood level with the first step of the down flight of steps.

Paul ran down the stairs. He was quiet about it, but the stair shaft itself was as silent as something that had been sealed for eternity. He made four floors without a hint of danger. Then, when he reached the landing of the fifth level below where he had started, he saw the staircase fire door closed, barring further progress.

He turned to the door leading out into the hallway of that level and went through it, onto soft carpeting.

"Mr. Formain?" asked a polite voice in his ear. "If you'll just come . . ."

A security agent, a young man by his voice, had been standing back by the side of the door where the latch was, his back to the wall alongside and waiting for Paul to come out. As Paul stepped through, the agent spoke and stepped forward to take hold of him. Paul felt the left hand of the other man expertly seeking the twin nerves just above his elbow and the man's right hand reaching out to catch his thumb and bend it back wristward in that unobtrusive hold long familiar to police people, known as the "come-along."

The searching hands of the security man failed of their mark, for no fault of the man himself, but for two reasons he could not have expected. The first was that his pinching left hand missed its mark completely, the seeking thumb and middle finger not finding the nerve-points they sought since they were hidden under the greatly overdeveloped muscles of Paul's arm, just above the elbow. The second was that Paul was no longer thinking his reactions out in conscious terms, but in this emergency abandoning himself to that invulnerable part of him that had earlier claimed his overdeveloped arm as its own. So, what actually happened was that even as the security man reached out to take him prisoner, even as he felt the man's hands upon him, Paul was already in movement.

At the other's touch, all in a split second, he checked, balanced, moved a fraction of an inch to the right, and drove the point of his elbow backward with all the unnatural strength of his arm.

It was a move executed with a hesitationless smoothness and accuracy that would have made it lethal against a trained fighter. It was aimed to be lethal. The elbow-point was fired with impossible accuracy into the unprotected area just below the man's breastbone, and driving upward. It would have torn lungs, crushed arteries, and possibly burst the heart. The only reason it did not do so, and did not kill, was that at the last split second Paul realized what was about to happen and managed to slightly deflect the aim.

Still, it lifted the man and slammed him back against the hallway wall, from which he fell forward and lay on his side, eyes half showing under fallen lids, legs a little drawn up and twitching with little spasmodic movements. Even as it was, he had been severely damaged.

And so almost, it seemed, had Paul.

It was nearly as if the blow he had just struck had recoiled on him with most of its original force. He doubled up as if he had been the target. A washback of emotion shuddered through his whole body, and he staggered blindly down the hall, dizzy, nauseated, half-blinded, and bent over. Still moving, however, he got himself under control. Somehow he sought for and found the control in him that was necessary, and it was like pushing a button. So swiftly that it almost seemed he had never felt it, the reaction vanished from him and he straightened up.

He found himself now at the end of the hall, by more all, curtained windows. The elevator tubes were close and there was no place else to go. He remembered that in case of trouble he was to seek out Kantele on the sixtieth level, and he stepped onto a disk floating up the up tube.

It carried him up with it. Over his head the bottom of the immediately superior disk closed him off into a little tube-shaped enclosure of which the bottom was his own disk, with him filling the tube. For the moment he was safe. Looking out through the transparent wall of the tube, he saw the various levels dropping past him, but though he saw occasional figures in the halls and standing by the tubes, none of them seemed to pay any special attention to him.

If the hotel security men were waiting for him anywhere, he thought, it would be at the roof-garden top of the hotel where the small-craft landing pad was. But that was thirty levels above the floor where he intended to get off.

He was at the fifty-eighth level now. He moved forward to the edge of the disk, and as the sixtieth level approached, he stepped off.

He stepped almost immediately into a hallway crowd of people coming and going, and standing around in small, talkative groups. He pushed his way through them and stepped into the first entrance to a banquet room he found. Within were tables at which chess matches were going on, here and there with a few watchers clustered around some special pair of players. Kantele was not in view. He left the room and went on.

In the third room he visited he found Kantele. She was with several other people who were watching an individual match across the room from the entrance, and not too far from the French windows which indicated an outside balcony or terrace beyond the banquet room. She was standing behind the chair of a man who, with a sudden quickening of his pulse, Paul recognized to be Blunt. Blunt sat leaning forward, absorbed in the condition of the board he was observing, and Kantele stood with one hand on his wide shoulder.

It occurred to Paul that he was going to have the chance of facing Blunt sooner than he had expected. H started toward the table where Blunt and Kantele watched, and abruptly stopped.

He no longer had the walking stick.

Paul stood still, and for a second the hum and movement of the room faded almost out of his consciousness. His hand was empty. But he could not remember either dropping the stick or laying it aside. All that occurred to him was that he must have let go of it in the reaction that followed his elbow-jabbing of the security man. Well, if that was the case, Blunt might have something to explain to the police—and then he might not. It might be that, as in the case of Tyne's visit to 2309, hotel security would, on finding the stick, politely cover up for him.

At any rate, Paul intended to face the Chantry Guild head *now*. Paul went forward again.

But he was already too late. Kantele, he found, had already looked up and seen him. Her face unnaturally expressionless, she shook her head at his advance and then gestured with a nod at the French windows. Paul hesitated for a second, then turned and obeyed.

He passed the tables and stepped through one of the French windows, closing it behind him. He found himself, as he had expected, on a long and fairly narrow terrace with a waist-high parapet of ornamental stone around it. Beyond the parapet he could see the rooftops of lower surrounding buildings, and beyond them the farther levels of Chicago Complex. The afternoon had turned out to be almost cloudless, and the bright sun lanced warmly across the white, round tables and translucent, single-legged chairs on the terrace. He walked to the parapet and looked over.

Below him the side of the Koh-i-Nor's North Tower fell sheer in an unbroken pattern of alternate window glass and marbled tile to the top level of commuter traffic, sixty stories below. Postage-stamp-size directly underneath him was the main concourse in front of the tower, and, a narrow two hundred yards away across it, some sort of office building with a single aircar on its landing pad, and the highly-polished surface of the building's construction tile reflecting the utter blue of the sky.

He turned back from the parapet. On the white table

top nearly beside him was a brightly-illustrated throwaway magazine left by some earlier visitor to the terrace. The breeze across the terrace ruffled and tried to turn its pages. He glanced at the titles in colorful type on its cover. The lead one jumped at him.

Was Gandhi's Way Right?

And under this, in slightly less bold print:

The Psychotics of Our Overcrowded Cities

The author of this later article, he noticed with interest, was the same Dr. Elizabeth Williams, psychiatrist, he had encountered only the week before.

He reached for the magazine to turn to the article.

"Formain," said a voice. He looked up and turned.

Facing him from about fifteen feet away, his hand on the half-open French door through which he must just have stepped out onto the terrace, was Butler. The small hotel security man stood with one hand thrust into the right pocket of his barrel-cut jacket. His face was as polite as ever.

"You better come along quietly with me, Formain," he said.

Paul let go of the magazine. The fingers of his single hand flexed reflexively. He took a casual step in Butler's direction.

"Stop there," said Butler. He took his hand out of his pocket, revealing a small finger gun. Paul stopped.

"Don't be foolish," said Paul.

Butler looked at him with the closest approach to a flicker of emotion in his face that Paul had yet seen.

"I think that's my line," Butler said. "Don't be foolish, Formain. Come along quietly."

Paul looked across the short distance separating them. His first impulse, as it had been with the agent in the hallway, had been to go into action. He had checked that. And now a part of him waited critically to see what the other part of him might do. He looked at Butler, trying to narrow down his mental field of vision. Trying to see the man as something individual, unique, limited by the forces that tied him into his environment, by the very elements that made him dangerous.

Anyone can be understood, Paul told himself. Anyone.

For a second, Butler's image seemed to swim in Paul's retina with the effort Paul was making, like a figure seen through the bottom of a drinking glass. Then the image cleared.

"I don't intend to be foolish," said Paul. He sat down on the edge of the table beside him. "I'm not going with you."

"Yes," said Butler. He held the finger gun steady.

"No," said Paul. "If you take me in, I'll tell the police that you were the source of supply for the drugs of the man in 2309. I'll tell them you used to be a drug addict yourself."

Butler gave a small, tired sigh.

"Come along, Formain," he said.

"No," said Paul. "To take me, you'll have to shoot me first. If you kill me, there's bound to be the kind of investigation you don't want. If you do less than kill me, I'll tell them what I just told you I'd say."

There was a moment's silence on the terrace. While it lasted, they could both hear the leaves of the magazine rustling in the breeze.

"I am not a drug addict," said Butler.

"No," said Paul. "But you were until some fanaticism, some particular blind faith gave you the strength to kick the habit. You're not afraid of the fact being found out so much as the fact that an investigation into the fact would cause you to be cut off from this source of strength. If I mention it, the police will have to investigate the matter. So, you're going to let me go."

Butler regarded him. The security man's expression was as unreadable as ever, but the finger gun jerked for a second as his hand trembled momentarily. He hid the hand back in the pocket of his jacket.

"Who told you?" he asked.

"You did," said Paul. "Being the sort of man you are, the rest had to follow."

Butler watched him for a second more, then turned toward the French door behind him.

"Someday I'll make you tell me who told you," he

said, and went back into the banquet rooms where the chessmen were at war.

The French door had barely closed behind him when one of the other doors opened and Kantele stepped through, quickly closing the door behind her. She came quickly over to Paul, her fine-cut features pale and her lips a little compressed above the square blue shoulders of her tailored jacket and the tooled-leather strap of the heavy handbag cutting into one of them.

"How did you—no, don't tell me," she corrected herself as she met him. "There isn't time. There are a dozen more hotel men going through the banquet rooms. Here . . ."

She lifted her large handbag onto one of the tables and pressed it at certain points. It opened out like a slow-motion jack-in-the-box. It was a one-man parachute copter, of the emergency type used by aircraft and fire departments. She unbuckled the straps that would fit around his shoulders and helped him into it.

"As long as the air-traffic police don't spot you, you'll be all right," she said, tightening the straps upon him. "Head for the rooftop of that building opposite."

The sound of one of the French doors opening made them both turn. It flew open, smashing against one of the tables, and two men catapulted onto the terrace, drawing guns from their jackets.

Paul did not hesitate. With one sweep of his powerful arm he snatched up the table alongside and threw it, as if it had been a balsa-wood mock-up of itself, at the two charging men.

They dodged, but not quickly enough. They went down before it. And Paul, sweeping Kantele up in his grasp, took one long step to the top of the parapet, and another off into sixty levels of emptiness.

Chapter 9

They fell like a stone, while Paul's hand, restricted by the fact that his arm must keep its hold on Kantele, fumbled with the controls of the parachute copter. He located them finally and switched them on, and suddenly it was like a heavy brake being applied against the force of gravity as the spinning blades blurred into action to break their fall.

"I'm sorry," he said to Kantele. "But they'd seen you with me. I couldn't leave you behind to face the music."

She did not answer. Her head lay back and sideways against his shoulder and her eyes were closed. Her face was like the face of someone who has surrendered completely to some superior force.

Paul turned his attention to guiding the copter toward the building across the concourse from the hotel. He was only partially successful. The copter, powerful enough to handle a two-hundred-and-fifty-pound individual, was fighting a losing battle in trying to uphold the combined weights of a man and woman both well above the average in size. They were drifting off and down at a long slant, the way the winged seed of a maple tree flutters to earth in fall winds.

"The rooftop, you said?" asked Paul. Her eyes remained closed. He joggled her a little. "Kantele!"

She opened her eyes, slowly.

"Yes," she said. "What's that noise?"

There were faint, piping noises around them. Looking back over his shoulder, Paul saw the two men he had bowled over with the table, leaning on the parapet with their forearms, almost casually. But the fists of both held dark objects. They were shooting at Paul and Kantele.

The anesthetic slivers of metal which were the missiles of their weapons could not be too accurate at the present and steadily increasing range. Air police were the greater danger. Paul fingered the controls and they rotated slowly through a hundred-and-eighty-degree angle.

To the north of them and about five hundred feet up, were two specks approaching rapidly. Kantele saw them as Paul did, but she said nothing.

"And after we land on the roof, what?" asked Paul. He looked down into her face. She had closed her eyes again.

"Jase is waiting, on the floor below." She answered almost dreamily, and her head was back against his shoulder again.

"The floor below?" Paul was puzzled and nearly provoked by her. She seemed to have given the matter completely over into his hands. "We haven't time for the roof. I'll try for a window."

"If he has it open," she said dreamily, without opening her eyes.

He understood what she meant. They were falling swiftly, even though at a slant. If Jason Warren did not see them coming and get the window open in time, they would most certainly smash themselves against the unbreakable glass, bending their copter blades and ending in an unchecked drop to the traffic level thirty or forty stories below. There would be no hope for them.

"He'll have it open," said Paul. She did not disagree.

The police cars were swelling in size visibly with the swiftness of their approach. But the building before them was close now, too. Looking down, Paul suddenly saw one of the top level's larger windows slide back.

He angled the copter toward it.

For a moment he thought that he would be falling too rapidly to make it over the open sill. Then it leaped up before him. He jammed the controls on to full braking power, ready to burn the copter's small motor out now that it had served its purpose.

The last burst of effort from the device saved them. The copter shot them through the window, checked itself in the midst of its own suddenly enclosed hurricane, and froze its bearings with an ear-splitting screech. Paul and Kantele dropped less than three inches to land on their feet, upright upon an office floor.

The hurricane with its floating documents and light objects blew itself suddenly out, and the Necromancer came toward the two of them from a far corner of the room. Kantele opened her eyes and looked about her; then, suddenly stiffening, pushed herself almost violently away from Paul and, turning her back, walked several steps from him until a desk blocked her path. Paul looked after her, frowning.

"Get that copter off," said Warren. But Paul was already shrugging out of the straps. The piece of ruined equipment fell heavily to the floor.

"Well, Jase?" asked Paul. The minute he had said it the name sounded oddly on his tongue. For the first time he realized that he had always thought of the Necromancer in terms of his last name. That he had called him by the name everybody else who knew him used, was like cracking a barrier. He saw the other man glance at him for a moment, oddly.

"We're located, now," said the man called Jase. "We're probably surrounded already. We'll have to take another way out with you."

"Why bother?" asked Paul. Jase looked at him again, oddly.

"We take care of our own people, of course," Jase said.

"Am I one?" asked Paul.

The Necromancer stopped dead and looked at him. "Don't you want to be?" he asked. He nodded toward the door of the office. He added, dryly, "If you want to walk out there, I won't stop you."

"...... Paul, and to his own surprise found himself smiling a little sadly, "no, I'm one of you, all right."

"Good." Jase turned briskly to a desk and swept it clean of papers, desk pad, and office instruments. "Shut the window," he said, and Kantele went across the room to it. As the window closed, Jase lifted a brief case from below the table and opened it.

He took from the brief case a large, hooded, black cloak which, when he put it on and pulled the hood over his head, covered him almost completely. In the shadow of the hood his face lost something of its identity. Kantele had come back to the table. He took also from the brief case what looked like three good-sized cones of incense, and lighted them. They immediately began to pour forth a dense, heavy smoke which quickly started to obscure the room. The smoke, to Paul's senses, had a sweet, almost cloying smell and evidently something narcotic about it, for he felt himself getting light-headed with the first few inhalations.

They were all standing close around the desk. The room was a fog of dark smoke now, in which Paul's drugged senses were already having difficulty focusing on nearby objects. Across the desk from him the Necromancer's voice came suddenly, deeper-toned than ordinary, measured, chanting. . . .

"This ae nighte, this ae nighte, everie night and alle . . ."

Kantele's voice, from another quarter of the table, chimed in. And what had been pure doggerel recital from Jase's lips acquired a touch of music with the addition of her voice.

"Fire and sleete and candlelight, destruction take these alle."

The Necromancer produced one more item and put it on the desk. At the sight of it Paul's mind went suddenly white with an awareness of danger. He would have been a poor sort of mining engineer not to have recognized it. What Jase had just put on the table was a cotton block of blasting jelly two inches on a side, enough to reduce the office and everyone within it to uncollectable fragments. It was topped with no more than a ninety-second fuse, and as Paul peered through the gathering smoke, the Necromancer pinched the fuse and started it burning.

Jase chanted alone:

"If from hence away thou'rt past"

And Kantele's voice joined him in chorus:

"Everie nighte and alle . . ."

"To Whinny-muir thou comest at last," Jase chanted alone.

"Destruction take thee alle." Kantele joined again.

He should not have recognized what they were chanting, but it happened that Paul did. From where or how it came to him, he could not in that smoke-fogged moment remember. But it was a somewhat changed version of one of the old north-of-England corpse chants, sung at wakes with the corpse under the table and a dish of salt on its breast. It was a ritual with its roots going back beyond Christianity to the ancient Celts, to a time when small dark men crept together in the forests to sing their dead kinsman on his road of shadows, in the first nights after his departure. And the version Paul heard now had none of the solemn music of its seventeenth-century shape, but was nearly back to the harsh atonal chant of the original primitive, cold as winter stones and unsparing as the wind across them. On it went, with Jase speaking alone and then Kantele joining in the chorus. It was a "lykewake dirge":

"If ever thou gavest roof and flame,

You don't start with True.
You change to True.

It happens after you've been smoking for a while. You decide it's time you changed to a low tar and nicotine cigarette. And that decision brings many people to True. Because True is not only gentle on your mind, it's gentle on your taste.

Shouldn't your next cigarette be True?

Regular: 11 mg. "tar", 0.7 mg. nicotine, av. per cigarette, FTC Report March '74.

Warning: The Surgeon General Has Determined That Cigarette Smoking Is Dangerous to Your Health.

You don't start with True.
You change to True.

It happens after you've been smoking other menthols for a while. You decide it's time you changed to a low tar and nicotine cigarette. And that decision brings many people to True Menthol. Because True is not only gentle on your mind, it's gentle on your taste.

Shouldn't your next menthol be True?

Menthol: 12 mg. "tar", 0.7 mg. nicotine, av. per cigarette, FTC Report March '74.

Everie nighte and alle . . .
Pass thee by the standing stane,
Destruction take thee alle.

"The standing stane, when thou art past,
Everie nighte and alle . . .
To empty airt thou comest fast,
Destruction take thee alle.

"If ever thou feddest fish or fowl,
Everie nighte and . . ."

Distantly, through the chanting and the swirling smoke, came the sound of a loud-speaker from beyond the closed window.

"Formain! Paul Formain! This is the police. We have you completely surrounded. If you do not come out within two minutes, and those with you, we will force an entrance." There was a momentary pause, and then the speaker once more rattled the window. "Formain! Paul Formain. This is the police. We have you. . . ."

Meanwhile, in the office the smoke was now so thick that even the cotton block of blasting jelly and its rapidly diminishing fuse was hidden from Paul's eyes. He seemed to hear the chanting of Jase and Kantele mounting in volume:

"From empty airt when thou'rt past
Everie nighte and alle . . .
To Alleman's Ende thou comest at last,
Destruction take thee alle."

Something was happening now. The fuse was shortening fast. A pressure was building up about the three of them and the desk between them. Paul felt a sudden deep-moving urge to join with Kantele in the chorus of the chant. He heard the fuse fizzing. A part of him shouted that in seconds he would be blown to pieces. But another part watched, detached and curious, and checked the chant in him before it reached his lips.

"And if thou holdest to any thinge
Everie nighte and alle . . .
The Ende thou canst not enter in,
Destruction take thee alle."

Jase's and Kantele's voices were all around Paul now, like a loop of rope holding them all together and drawing tighter. The fuse must be all burned down now.

"But if thou guardest nae thing at all,
Everie nighte and alle . . .
To Alleman's Ende thou'lt passe and falle
And Destruction'll take thee alle!"

Suddenly, Jase and Kantele were gone, and almost in the same fraction of a second the world lighted up around Paul and he felt the sudden slam of enormous pressure against him, as if he were a fly clapped between two giant hands. He was aware, for one tiny moment of perception, of the office flying to pieces around him as the blasting jelly exploded, and then he himself seemed to fly off into nothingness.

Book Two: SET

> *By stony staircase, hall, and pier,*
> *Those shadows mazed around me there,*
> *Wove doubt on doubt, and—fools!—broke out*
> *That part in me that feared no doubt.*
> THE ENCHANTED TOWER

Chapter 10

With the situation fully and correctly understood, it becomes entirely reasonable that the very small fraction of a second preceding a violent death could be a trigger to speculative thought.

Ninety-three years after Paul was caught by the explosion of the block of blasting jelly, the phenomenon of *no-time*—that is, of a state of existence in which time is lacking—was finally and fully explained. It had been made use of, of course, even by people preceding the Chantry Guild. On a hit-and-miss basis. But with the development of the phase-shift form of transportation that permitted the interstellar expansion of the human race, it became necessary to understand the a-time state which was basic to the phase shift. Briefly and crudely, the explanation was that there is a reciprocal relationship between time and position. And if time becomes nonexistent (perhaps *nonoperative* would be a better word) then the choice of position becomes infinite.

There are, of course, practical difficulties limiting th use of this, which arise when the problem of exactly ca culating the desired position arises. But that has been explained earlier in a different place.* Once more, in the future and again in a different place, the problem of no-time will be entered into once again when the philosophical aspects of it become relevant. But for now, to return once more to the historical moment of the exploding blasting-jelly cube, the important thing is that for vulgar practical purposes, no-time can be taken merely to mean sufficient, uncounted time.

No one—literally, *no one*—is immune to error. It had been an error for Paul to linger behind Jase and Kantele in their departure and be caught by the first edge of the explosion. Having been caught, there was only one way out. He went instinctively into no-time to escape being destroyed, as lesser individuals have done before him. Nearly everyone has heard of the authenticated instance of the man who walked around the horses of his coach into nonexistence, and there are many others.

In no-time he remained conscious, and was triggered into a sudden awareness that since the original boating accident, at no time had he ever been without some element of awareness. Even his sleep had been given over either to periods of asymbolic thought on the subconscious level or to dreams. And his dreams, in fact, seemed a fine mill in the complex of his mental machinery. A mill which took the results of the crude data that had been mined from the solid substances of his daytime surroundings by the tools of his senses, then rough-crushed by the intellectual upper processes of his intelligence, and now were ground to fine powders and begun on the obscurer process that would separate out the pure valuable elements of comprehension.

Other than this he did not approach any letting go of his awareness. It had occurred to him that this might be the basic cause of his unyielding refusal to accept hypnosis. But this explanation failed to completely satisfy him in that area of his perception in which he was most sensitive—it did not *feel* like the complete answer. If he recognizable processes by which he attempted to understand and control his environment could be compared to the mechanical, this last could be best compared to something chemical. And this was so powerful and effective a tool in its own way that for practical purposes it blinded him to the common channels of reasoning. It was extremely difficult for him to add two and two and get four. It was exceedingly simple and natural for him to contemplate two by itself, as an isolated element, and find four as an implied, characteristic possibility of it.

He looked out on all existence through a window that revealed only unique elements. He approached everything in terms of isolates. Isolates and their implied possibilities of characteristics. All time, for example, was implied in any single moment that he might choose to examine. But the moment itself was unique and unalterably separated from any other moment, even though the other moment also implied all of time.

It followed that it was almost impossible for him to be tricked or lied to. Any falsity palmed off on him almost immediately collapsed like fraudulently understrength construction under the natural weight of its own proliferating possibilities. It also followed, and this was not always an advantage, that he was almost impossible to surprise. Any turn of events, being implied in the moment preceding its taking place, seemed perfectly natural to him. As a result he did not question a great many things that he might normally have been expected to question.

He had not, therefore, questioned the abilities the Chantry members seemed to claim for themselves. It had seemed—to this part of him, at least—quite reasonable that Jase and Kantele should attempt to make their escape with him by means of narcotic smoke, archaic corpse chant, and a block of blasting jelly with a short fuse. He had, however, allowed himself to get so interested in what was going on that he found himself left behind and caught in the first microsecond of the explosion.

He was driven out to the very edges of his consciousness, but no farther. He was aware of himself moving very swiftly and at the same time being driven by the explosion away down into the impossibly tiny end of something like an enormous funnel. He flew through this into all but complete unconsciousness, fighting for survival. He was an infinity of fathoms deep in darkness, but somewhere above him was light and life.

He came up, fighting.

His mind was quicker to react to full consciousness again than his body. He woke to find himself plunging clear across some sort of small, bare room with a circular, raised stage in the center of it, and carrying four men along with him as they attempted to restrain him. He was headed for the door to the room.

He checked, understanding. And, after a second, the man holding on to him let go. As they cleared away from in front of him, Paul caught sight of himself in the mirror surface of a far wall. His clothes were torn, apparently by the explosion, and his nose was bleeding slightly. He got a handkerchief tissue from his pocket and wiped the blood away from his upper lip. The nose stopped bleeding. Jase and Kantele watched him from across the room.

"I don't understand this," said one of the men who had been holding him, a small, brisk-looking man with a shock of brown hair over a sharp-featured face. He looked at Paul almost challengingly. "How did you get here? If Jase brought you, why didn't you come with Jase?"

Paul frowned.

"I seem to have been a little slow," he said.

"Never mind," spoke up Jase from across the room. "If you're all right now, Paul, come on."

He led the way out of the room, Kantele following with a momentary, troubled glance in Paul's direction. Paul went after them.

He caught up with them in a hall outside the room. It was a blank wall without windows, and it led them up an incline until they stepped suddenly around a corner and emerged into open air. Paul looked curiously around himself. They had emerged onto a vast field spotted with the raised white concrete pads from which space-going vehicles fitted with their great collars of lifting equipment took off. Beyond were the snow-topped peaks of a mountain range Paul did not recognize.

It was no commercial field. The uniformity of the constructions about the field and the khaki coveralls of the personnel about spoke clearly to the effect that this was a government installation.

"Where are we?" asked Paul. But Jase was already striding away with Kantele to a pad occupied by the squat, almost bulbous shape of an outer-space vessel looking like an ancient artillery shell many times enlarged, and fitted with its spreading soup-plate collar of atmosphere engines, ducted fans in the outer ring, ramjets in toward the center. Paul caught up with Jase and Kantele.

"Where are we?" he asked again.

"Tell you after we're aboard," said Jase economically. They walked along together, Jase staring straight ahead toward the ship, his face like a knife edge, Kantele with her wordless gaze down and ahead, so that she looked at the treated gravel surface of the field on which no green grew, just before her as she walked. Paul felt a sudden small rush of sorrow that human beings should be so locked away and separate in their body and mind, so bound to different wheels. And, with a sudden soundless shock, it occurred to him that out of all the real universe the one class of isolates who strove and threatened to burst the bounds of their separateness was people.

This realization, simple as it appeared in bald statement, exploded in Paul like a pan of flash powder set off before a man in a vast and complex city, standing lightless under the stars. It blinded, rather than illuminated, but its light left an afterimage printed on the retinas of the explorer in the dark, and would be permanently remembered. With his mind washed clean of other matters for the moment, Paul walked automatically into the base tunnel of the take-off pad, rode the elevator up through pad and collar, and paid little attention to anything until the whine of the outer ring of fans began to impinge on his consciousness. He came back to present awareness to see that he was seated in a convertible acceleration couch-chair, in a passenger compartment of the ship. In front of him he could see the black top of Jase's head just showing above the top cushion of the next couch-chair, and across the aisle from Jase, up agains' the rounded wall enclosing the elevator-tunnel running up the center of the ship, he saw the profile of Kantele.

The ship lifted. After a little the sound of the fans was drowned out in the beginning thunder of the jets, which mounted the ladder of volume into silence. A little after that, the viewing tank in the wall beside Paul lighted up, and, looking into this illusion of a window, he saw the lifting collar of atmosphere engines, their earth-bound clumsiness all left behind, fall away gracefully like some enormous soaring bird toward the cloud-laced earth far below.

"Couchback, all passengers," announced a speaker system somewhere above Paul's head. "All passengers, couchback now."

The chairs tilted and leveled into horizontal position. Deep cushioning buffers moved in about his body. There was a moment of silence and then the space engines fired, and their mighty thrust threw the blunt body of the ship, with Kantele, and Jase, and Paul, and all within it, out between the stars.

Mercury, Paul discovered, was a five-day run. The ship had four cross levels between the pilot room in the nose and the engines in the rear. The passengers were restricted to two of them. Evidently because it was government procedure, they were required to take mild sedatives during the actual flight. These made Kantele and three other passengers whom Paul did not know sleepy. They spent most of their time dozing with their couch-chairs in a reclining position. Jase had disappeared early up into the crew's section and Paul had not seen him after that for the first four days of the run. Since Kantele seemed to reinforce the effect of her sedatives with an obvious disinclination to have anything to do with Paul, once more that left Paul solitary.

To Paul's unusual set of mental and physical reactions, the sedatives brought a bodily lethargy, but an increase in mental speculation and introspection. Jase had escaped early before Paul could question him again, but a tall, stiff-backed man, in the seat behind Paul and across the aisle which with the two rows of seats circled the central elevator shaft, had replied to Paul's question.

"Operation Springboard," he had said sharply. He

stared almost fiercely at Paul out of middle-aged eyes
above a neat white mustache that contrasted with the
brown tan of his face. "You know about the project to
reach the Arcturian planets, don't you? Apprentice, are
you?"

"Yes," said Paul.

"Ask your master, boy! He'll answer you. Who is he?
Necromancer Warren?"

Secretly a little amused to be addressed as "boy," a
term he had not had used to him since he was fourteen,
Paul nodded.

"That's right," he said. "Do you happen to be a
Necromancer, too?"

"No, no," said the man. "Sociologist—what they call
'untitled.' Don't have the patience for the rigmarole. But
it's fine work for a younger man like yourself to get into."
He grew fiercer, suddenly. The white mustache seemed
to bristle. "A good work!"

"Necromancy?" asked Paul.

"All of it. All of it. Think of our children . . . and their
children."

A man of about the same age as the white-mustached
speaker leaned out of a couch-chair farther back on
Paul's side of the circular aisle.

"Heber," he said.

"Yes, yes," said the white-mustached man, sinking
back into his seat. "You're right, Tom. Don't ask me
questions, boy; ask your master. I've got to take my
medication now, anyway." He reached into the little compartment in one arm of his chair, and Paul, giving up
that avenue of information, turned and sat back in his
own place.

He had plenty to occupy his mind. He let his attention
go free among it.

It was a type of mental activity having its own element of actual built-in pleasure reward, a pleasure to
which, he had lately come to realize, it would be quite
possible to become addicted, if it were not for the fact
that the basic drive to accomplish forbade too much
loitering on the pathway from means to end. It was the
sheer pleasure of turning the questioning spirit loose in
the great dark city of all personal knowledge. For those

who panicked easily in the dark, it was no occupation. But for those without fear and the true night-sight of understanding, there was no pleasure like that of wandering some strange and intricate part of that city, until out of shadow rose shapes, and out of shapes, plan, and out of plan—original purpose. Only then, at last with original purpose encompassed and understood, came—perhaps—the greater occupation of putting that knowledge to work in new building.

So for five days Paul all but lost himself in a new part of his city of knowledge. It was only shortly before landing on Mercury that he was abruptly called back from it, and the one who called him back was Kantele.

"I wasn't going to ask you why," she said. He awoke to the fact that she was standing in the aisle before his seat, looking down at him. "But I just can't. . . . Why did you do it? Why did you have to kill Malorn?"

"Kill who?" asked Paul. For a second she and her question were still mixed in with the shapes of his thoughts. Then the shapes faded and he became aware that they were, at least as far as he could see on this side of the elevator shaft, alone on the level among the couch-chairs.

"Kevin Malorn—the man at the hotel."

"Kevin Malorn," echoed Paul. For a part of a second the only thing that was in his mind was a feeling of unutterable sadness that he should have been the instrument of the man's death and never until now known the name under which other people had known him alive.

"You won't tell me," said Kantele, when he did not answer immediately. He looked up at her pale, set face.

"Yes," he said. "But you probably won't believe me. I didn't kill him. I don't know why he died."

She stared at him for a moment longer, then whirled about and walked off around the elevator tube. Following a little later, he discovered all the other passengers one level up in the lounge, watching in the large tank there the ascent of the landing collar, with chemical engines fueled by native Mercury products, that would carry them safely down to that planet's surface.

Chapter 11

It was a strange tumbled landscape through which they all walked the half mile from the ship to the reception dome of Station Springboard. The sky was white to the right and dark to the left, and cloudless. There was enough of an atmosphere here on the surface of Mercury's twilight zone to scatter the light in this direction. The resulting illumination seen through the face windows of Paul's protective suit was like the yellow glare before a thunderstorm back under the kinder sky of Earth. In this all-pervasive, unchanging light, the terrain appeared to be peopled with the split and damaged fragments of fantastic sculptures. It would be the temperature changes of alternating dark-side and light-side storms that had caused this, and the volcanic action along the line of weakness in Mercury's crust that the Twilight Zone represented. But still it looked like a country out of a dream of unreality, a garden out of a nightmare, set up and despoiled by witches.

They entered the dome and stepped through a lock into an elevator which sank for a quite noticeable distance. Paul guessed that he might now be in the neighborhood of forty to sixty levels underground, for the elevator had been a large mechanical, rather than magnetic, one, and the descent had been uncomfortably swift. As the elevator halted, a further door opened and they passed into a desuiting room.

From the desuiting room they were herded into separate cubicles for what Jase informed Paul were purposes of decontamination. Paul found himself instructed by a wall speaker to strip, pass through a shower area, and a further door where new clothes for him would be waiting.

He did so and came out into another cubicle, this one not much more than an area hacked out of the solid granitic rock. On a concrete bench there a pile of clothing was waiting for him.

He set about putting it on and found it to be of a

peculiar style. There were soft leather shoes, pointed at
the toe, fawn-colored; what seemed to be long green
stockings; shorts; a green smock with a loose belt to
cinch it up, and a sort of half-sleeved leather jacket.

It seemed likely to Paul that the Chantry Guild was
given to dressing for dinner, so to speak, here on Mercury. He put the clothes on—the left arm of smock
and jacket had been designed sleeveless and all the
clothes were in his size—and stepped through the further
door of the second cubicle.

He checked instinctively.

He had emerged into a single, low-ceilinged room,
crudely hollowed out of the rock and lighted by two
flaring torches in heavy wall brackets of some metal-like
blackened iron. The floor itself was roughhewed of rock
and pressed hard against the soles of his feet through the
soft leather of his shoes. Beyond the torches was darkness and he could see no far wall.

He turned quickly, back the way he had come. And
stopped. There was no door behind him, through where
he had stepped a minute before. He faced more of the
hewn-rock wall, only that. He reached out and touched
it with his hand. It felt as solid as judgment day.

He turned back to the light of the torches. Between
them now, he saw standing the man called Heber, the
torchlight sparkling on his white mustache. Unlike Paul,
he was clothed in a single scarlet robe and hood. The
hood threw a shadow across his forehead and the long
sleeves of the robe fell together from his hands, which
were joined together before him.

"Come here," said Heber. His lips trembled a second
after the last word, as if he could just barely restrain himself from adding "boy!" Paul walked up to him and
stopped. Heber was looking past him, the older man's
shadowed eyes seeming fantastically deep-socketed in
the shadow of the hood.

"I am here to sponsor this apprentice," announced
Heber, "to his initiation into the Société Chanterie. It is
required that there be two sponsors, one visible and
one invisible. Is the other sponsor here?"

"I am," said the voice of Jason Warren, startlingly at
Paul's right ear. He turned and saw nothing but the wall.

of the room. But he could now feel the presence of Jase beside him.

Paul turned back to Heber. The white-mustached man, he saw, was now holding in one arm a heavy, leather-bound, archaic-looking book. In the other hand he held by the middle a snake about four feet in length, which twisted and writhe'

"To the jurisdiction of the Alternate Laws you have come," said Heber. "To the jurisdiction of the Alternate Laws are you now committed and sealed. And to the jurisdiction of the Alternate Laws will you be bound, for all time past or present, and beyond time until the Alternate Laws cease their effect."

"I witness this," said the voice of Jason, at Paul's shoulder.

"Take then your spear," said Heber. He held out the snake toward Paul's single hand. Paul reached for it, but at the first touch of his fingers around it, it ceased suddenly to move and live. He found himself holding, in fact, a tall wooden spear with a dully gleaming metal point.

"Take then your shield," said Heber, stepping forward with the book. But it was a kite-shaped metal shield, with leather grips riveted to a wooden frame, that he hung from Paul's armless left shoulder by a wide leather strap.

"Now follow me," said Heber. He strode off into the darkness beyond the torches. And Paul, following after, found himself proceeding down slanted tunnels and around corners in the rock until he came finally to a small, square, carved-out room where two more torches burned on either side of what looked like a stone altar, more long than wide. Along the top of the altar were laid out, from left to right, a small toy sailboat with the tiny figure of the toy sailor within it spilled out as the boat lay over on one side, a toy model of the console of a mine, a stained and weathered conch shell, and a three-dimensional snapshot of the head of Malorn, the dead drug addict, showing the broken skull.

Heber and Paul stopped before the altar.

"Let the other sponsor now instruct the apprentice," he

said. Jase's voice spoke from Paul's other side. He looked at empty air.

"The apprentice is an apprentice in the art of Necromancy," his voice said. "Therefore we have brought him to the root of the tree. Let the apprentice look."

Paul turned his attention back to the altar. A massive tree root now emerged from the rock and arched out over the objects on the altar, down to his feet and Heber's.

"This," said the voice of Jase, "is the well Hvergelmer, in the realm of death. The root is the first root of the ash, Yggdrasil, which is the tree of life, knowledge, fate, time, and space. During the period of his vigil here, it is the duty of the apprentice to defend it, and the parts of his life which are on the altar. It may be that the apprentice will not be attacked during his time of vigil. But it may be that the dragon Nidhug and his brood will come to gnaw at the root of the tree. If the tree and the parts of his life are attacked, the apprentice may call on the Alternate Forces or not, as he chooses; but if he does not conquer Nidhug, Nidhug will devour him."

Jase ceased speaking. Heber spoke, and Paul turned his head to the white-mustached man.

"The tree," said Heber solemnly, "is an illusion. Life is an illusion. Nidhug and his brood are an illusion, as is all the universe, eternity, and time. Only the Alternate Forces exist, and time, space, and all things within them are merely toys of the Alternate Forces. Know this and know yourself unconquerable."

"You shall keep vigil," put in the sound of the Necromancer's voice, "until the third sounding of the gong. With the third sounding of the gong, you will be freed from the realm of death, back to the world of light and life once more. Now I leave you, until the third ringing of the gong."

Paul felt a void suddenly beside him. He turned instinctively toward Heber. The white-mustached man was still standing beside him.

"I leave now, too," said Heber. "Until the gong rings for the third time." He stepped past Paul, back toward the entrance to the room; and as he did, Paul caught the ghost of a wink from the man's near eye, and a *sotto voce* mutter, "Rigmarole."

Then Heber was gone.

Silence held the room.

It was the silence of the rock where the rock is igneous in nature and far below ground. Here there was no water dripping, only the still cold. Even the torches flared in silence. Paul's breath went out in a frosty plume in that red, dancing light, and vanished with each fresh inhalation.

But he began to become aware.

About him was stone, the mineral flesh of Mercury, in all directions. The rough, cut stone underfoot pressed sharply against his feet, the cold wrapped him like a chilly cloak. The minutes passed in solemn procession, all but identical one with the other. Time piled up in the quiet of the room, the strap of the shield cut into his shoulder and his fingers grew a little cramped around the wooden shaft of the spear. He held it with its butt on the floor, its point elevated, angled a little out from him like a Roman sentry. An hour went by, and then another. And then, perhaps, another. . . .

The solemn, brassy note of a deep gong struck once, reverberated through the entrance to the room, and beat about his ears. It rang away into silence, leaving a memory behind it in the noiselessness of the room until that, too, was buried and smoothed over by the marching minutes.

Paul's mind drifted out to an unconscionable distance. He leaned on his spear, now, and the shield had swung forward with its own weight. He thought of mountains whose stony sides and slopes were constructed of empty space, and of the twinkling illuminations of distant habitations upon the mountain peaks, which were the lights of the farther stars, stars not seen from Earth. A bittersweet emotion of sorrow and desire stirred in him like faint smoke from burning incense. Love and hunger pulled against each other within him. . . .

And then suddenly, distant in the back of his mind, came a chime of warning.

He came back to the stony room. It was as it had been

before. The torches still flared upward and his breath
smoked peacefully on the still air. But now there was
something more. While he had daydreamed, the deep
waters of some unseen danger had welled up to the
very entrance of the room. It lapped now in the darkness
just beyond the reach of his sight. And in those deep
waters, there was something stirring.

It was Nidhug and his scaly brood.

They were not real. They were an illusion, as was the
deep mass of waters making a beleaguered island of this
room. Paul recognized this with a sure and certain swiftness. Those minds among the Chantry Guild who were
capable of such tricks were flooding the solid (but to
these productions of their minds, transparent) rock with
the emanations of fear, pictured as heavy, secret waters.
And through the fear, in the guise of a monstrous, scaly
worm and its litter, they were now lifting the image of
self-doubt. These things were fantasies, but nonetheless
dangerous. Fear can be a deadly danger to the mind, and
self-doubt can cause an organism to destroy itself, as
Paul knew. Knowledge could be a shield and wisdom a
weapon, but it took something uniquely human to use
them.

He braced himself. The rising tide of fear was already
flooding into the room. If he allowed his senses to yield
to the fantasy, he could see it, like a gray, quicksilver
tide, pushing its sullen rivulets into this and that small
indentation in the rough floor. Nidhug and his children
were very close.

The gong rang for a second time.

The waters crested suddenly, swirling into the room.
They mounted up to his knees, surged to his waist, and
in seconds eddied about his throat. They swelled over
his head. And touched the ceiling. The room was drowned.

One massive body length below the unblocked opening
of the room, Nidhug gave his final surge of approach. He
lifted like a demon out of darkness, and a second later
his hideous mask blocked the entrance to the room.

Leveling his spear, hunching his shoulder behind the
shield, Paul went to meet him. As in a nightmare, the
heavy waters of fear slowed his thrust to a dreamlike
slowness. The point of his spear slid deliberately through

the impeding medium and glanced off the tortured dragon-face.

But the overdeveloped muscles of Paul's arm, like what they represented in Paul himself, were something more than ordinary strength. The spear point, glancing off, dug a deep furrow from the twisted jaw to the staring eyes, and a flood of deep, luminescent, reddish blood stained and clouded the atmosphere of the room.

In this murk the battle became obscure. It became drearily a matter of Paul's thrusting back what came at him again and again. Gradually there broke on him the understanding that this was a contest that he perpetuated by the very act of fighting in it. The way to victory here was to deny the enemy. He laughed.

He threw away both shield and spear.

Like an express train, Nidhug leaped upon him. Paul stood still. And the gaping jaws, monstrous before him, closed as if on the invisible substance of an inch-thick wall between them. And the creature vanished.

The waters began to slowly ebb from the room. Far away the first shivering sounds of the third striking of the gong reached out to Paul's ears.

And in that moment, that tiny piece of a second, with the dragon vanished and the waters failing, something real and deadly reached through and struck.

It came from a distance which compared to the distance to the farthest stars was like a step to a long day's journey. It came with a speed beside which the speed even of thought was too slow to be measurable. It came along the dark and cobbled road of which Paul had dreamed on returning to the hotel after he had first seen Jase. It was blind and young and not yet fully formed, but it recognized its still-unarmored foe by sure instinct. And it struck.

It brought Paul to his knees as a giant might strike down a baby with a sword of steel—but it clashed like steel on steel against his invincible self behind. For a moment the forces hung together, and then the crest wave of the sounding gong finished closing the door through which the unknown had reached for a micro-second, for almost no time at all. And Paul knelt, free, but numb and blinded on the hard rock floor.

Paul's sight returned to show him the white ceiling of a room above the cot on which he lay. He was vaguely aware that they had carried him here.

Jase's face loomed over him. It was as keenly honed as ever, but there was a touch of friendliness there Paul had not seen before. Beside him was the white-mustached face of Heber showing concern.

"Quite a reaction you had there," said Jase, "after it was all over. We didn't expect to see you go down like that."

Paul focused on the Necromancer.

"You didn't?" he said. He frowned. "You certainly didn't expect me to stay on my feet?"

It was Jase's turn to frown, slightly.

"Why not?" he said. "If you'd stood up to things while it was going on, why collapse after it's all over?"

Paul faced it then. Jase and the other watchers had remained unaware. He closed his eyes wearily and a little bitterly, for he felt the beginnings of some sort of understanding seep into him at last; and understanding, he was discovering, like money, does not always bring happiness.

"Of course. Why not?" he agreed. "You must be right. I'm still suffering from the reaction."

Chapter 12

Dressed in ordinary jacket and slacks, one week later Paul sat with three other journeymen Chantry Guild members in a conference room of the orthodox part of Station Springboard. Talking to them was a brisk athletic young man with a short haircut and no older than Paul. Younger, in fact, than two of the journeymen, who looked disconcertingly like overfed salesmen in their thirties, except that one, who smelled strongly of after-shaving lotion, was twice as tall as the other.

"You can't *teach* the Alternate Laws," the instructor had begun by saying, as he half-perched on the edge of a table, facing the low, comfortable chairs in which the four sat. "Any more than you can *teach* the essential ability to create art, or the essential conviction of a religious belief. Does that make sense to you?"

"Ah, teaching!" said the fourth member of the journey-men group, a pleasant-faced, brown-headed young man, in an entirely unexpected, bell-toned bass. "What crimes have been committed in thy name!"

Since he had not spoken previously, the rest—even including the instructor—appeared somewhat startled, not only by his pronouncement, but by the volume and timbre of it. The young man smiled at them.

"True enough," said the instructor, after a slight pause. "And very true to the Alternate Laws. Let's simplify the Laws to a ridiculous extreme and say that the point they express is that as a rule of thumb, if it works best one way for everybody else, chances are that way won't be the best for you. In other words, if you want to get to the top of a mountain and you see a broad, well-marked, much-traveled road headed straight for it, the last route you should choose to the top of the mountain would be up that road."

He stopped talking. They all looked at him expectantly.

"No," he said, "I'm not going to tell you why. That would be teaching. Teaching is good only for learners, not for discoverers. Right now is the one and only time in the Chantry Guild that you're going to encounter anything like a question-and-answer period." He looked them over. "You're at liberty to try and tell *me* why, if you want to."

"Ah," said the large salesman sort with the shaving-lotion smell. He got the interjection out hurriedly, and it was at once noticeable to all his audience that his voice, though loud and determined, was neither bass nor bell-toned. "I—ah—understand that the Alternate Laws are parapsychological in nature. Can it be that involvement with the ordinary, that is to say—ah—scientific, laws has an inhibiting effect upon the person's—I mean the different sort of person who is able to take advantage of the powers of the Alternate Forces?" He drew a quick breath and added quickly, "I mean, his essential difference, so to speak?"

"No," said the instructor, kindly.

"No? Oh," said the other. He sat back, cleared his throat, crossed his legs, got out a handkerchief, and blew his nose loudly.

"The area of parapsychology," said the instructor, "is only a small part of the universe of time and space. The Alternate Laws cover all this and more."

"They mean what they say, don't they?" asked the smaller salesman-type unexpectedly. "Alternate Laws—other laws. And the only way to find the other ways is by deliberately avoiding the established way."

"That's right," said the instructor.

"Creative," rang the young man with the bass voice.

"And that's very right," said the instructor. He ran his glance from right to left over them. "None of you here would have got this far if you hadn't each demonstrated some capability in the area of the Alternate Laws. That capability may be parapsychological—say, teleportation. Or it might be an ability to write truly creative poetry, say. It might even be a particular sensitivity to the needs of growing plants. Not that I mean to give you the impression that creativity is all of the Alternate Laws, or even the key to them."

"Ah," said the large salesman, uncrossing his legs determinedly, "you certainly don't expect us just to write poetry or grow plants, or even teleport."

"No," said the instructor.

"Then—ah—can it be that you mean," said the large salesman, perspiration beginning to stand out on his brow, "that these things—whatever they may be—are a part, only a part, of the Alternate Laws? And it's the rest we have to go after? We have to try? We have to get?"

"Yes," said the instructor. "That's very good. It's not a full answer by any means——"

"No, no, of course not," said the large salesman, flushing and smiling, and pulling out his handkerchief. He blew his nose again as if it were a soldier's bugle.

"—a full answer by any means," said the instructor. "In fact, if there is a full answer, I don't know it. Everyone, in this, is on his own. And now," he said, standing up, "I think you've already had enough discussion about an inherently undiscussable subject to last you a lifetime. If indeed we haven't already done the damage of setting up some artificial concepts. Remember"—his whole voice and manner changed abruptly; it was almost as if he had reached out and wrapped some invisible cloak about him —"life is an illusion. Time and space and all things are an illusion. There is nothing, nothing but the Alternate Laws."

He ceased speaking suddenly. The journeymen got up automatically and began to file out. As Paul walked past, however, he felt his arm touched by the instructor.

"Just a minute," the instructor said. Paul turned. The other waited until the three other journeymen were out of the room. "You didn't say anything at all."

"Yes," said Paul. "That's right. I didn't."

"Mind if I ask why?"

"If I remember rightly," Paul said, "the key word of Walter Blunt's book is *destruct*."

"Yes, it is."

"And we," said Paul, looking down at the instructor from his own greater height, "were talking about creativity."

"Mmm," said the instructor, nodding his head thoughtfully, "I see. You think somebody's lying?"

"No," said Paul. He felt a sudden weariness that was not physical at all. "It's just that there was nothing to say."

The instructor stared at him.

"Now you're the one who's baffling me," the instructor said. "I don't understand you."

"I mean," said Paul patiently, "that it's no use saying anything."

The instructor shook his head again.

"I still don't understand you," he said. "But that's all right." He smiled. "In the Guild it's: To thine own self be true, thou needst not then explain to any man."

He patted Paul on the shoulder.

"Go, man!" he said, and on that note they parted.

Returning to his room, as Jase had warned him to do when not otherwise occupied, Paul passed along the catwalk above the relay room in the orthodox part of the Station. He had only a vague notion of what went on in the three-step accelerator that stretched through nearly a quarter mile of the vast cavern five levels high, with thirty- and forty-foot banks of equipment surrounding its tube shape. From news and magazine accounts he had acquired the general knowledge that its function was a matter of shuttling a point of higher-level energy back and forth along a line of constantly lower energy until the point's speed was just under the speed of light. At which time it "broke" (i.e., disappeared) and became instead a point of no-time, following the same path. This point of no-time, if perfectly synchronized with a point of no-time back in the laboratory building of World Engineer's Headquarters Complex, created a path for instantaneous, timeless transmission between the two points.

Since the point of no-time had universal dimension, it could, by a complicated technical process, be used to transport objects of any size from the primary station on the Earth to the secondary station here on Mercury Station. For some reason there had to be a critical minimum distance between stations—Mars and Venus were too close to Earth. Stations there had been tried and had failed. But theoretically at least, by this method Springboard could have been directly supplied from World Engineer's Complex, with anything it needed. It was not, in practice, because its function on Mercury was to tinker and experiment with its end of the transmission path. Instead, most of the Station's solid needs were met by resolution of materials from Mercury's crust.

It was also not only theoretically possible, but practically possible, to send living creatures including humans by the same route. However, those who tried it flirted with insanity or death from psychic shock, and even if they missed both these eventualities, could never be induced to try it again. Apparently what was experienced by the transmittee was a timeless moment of complete consciousness in which he felt himself spread out to infinite proportions and then recondensed at the receiving end. It did no good to use present known sedatives or anesthetics—these merely seemed to insure a fatal level of shock. Medicine was reported working on a number of drugs that showed some promise, but no immediate hope of discovering a specific was in sight.

Meanwhile drone ships had been started off at sublight velocities for some of the nearer stars known to have surrounding systems. The ships bore automatic equipment capable of setting up secondary receiving stations on their arrival on some safe planetary base. If and when medicine came through, the transportation setup would be already established.

All of this touched Paul only slightly. He recognized it and passed on, noting only that in passing by and over the equipment, as he was doing now, he received from it an emanation of mild, pleasurable excitement. Like the so-called "electric" feeling in the air before a thunderstorm, which comes not only from an excess of ions, but from the sudden startling contrast of dark and light, from the black thunderheads piling up in one quarter of a clear sky, the mutter and leap of sheet lightning and thunder along the cloud flanks, and the sudden breath and pause of cooler air in little gusts of wind.

He passed on and entered the area of smaller corridors and enclosures. He passed by the double airlock doors of the transparent enclosure that held the swimming pool. With the relative preciousness of water, this had been set up as a closed system independent of the rest of the station and supplied with a certain amount of artificial gravitation for Earth-normal swimming and diving. Kantele was all alone in the pool. As he passed, he saw her go gracefully off the low board. He paused to watch her swim, not seeing him, to the side of the pool just beyond the glass where he stood. She did not look so slim in a bathing suit, and for a moment a deep sensation of loneliness moved him.

He went on, before she could climb out of the pool and see him. When he got to his room there was a notice attached to the door: "Orientation. Room eight, eighteenth level, following lunch, 1330 hours."

Orientation took place in another conference room. The man in charge was in his sixties and looked and acted as if he had been on an academic roster for some time. He sat on a small raised stage and looked down at Paul, the three men who had been with him for the meeting with the instructor on the subject of Alternate Laws, and six other people, of whom one was a young woman just out of her teens, not pretty, but with an amazingly quick and cheerful expression. The man in charge, who introduced himself as Leland Minault, did not begin with a lecture. Instead he invited them to ask him questions.

There was the usual initial pause at this. Then one of the five men Paul had not met before spoke up.

"I don't understand the Chantry Guild's connection with Project Springboard and the Station, here," he said. Leland Minault peered down at the speaker as if through invisible spectacles.

"That," said Minault, "is a statement, not a question."

"All right," said the speaker. "Is the Chantry Guild responsible for Station Springboard, or the work on a means of getting out between the stars?"

"No," said Minault.

"Well then," asked the other, "just what are we doing here, anyway?"

"We are here," said Minault deliberately, folding both hands over a slight potbelly, "because a machine is not a man—beg pardon"—he nodded at the one woman in the group—"human being. A human being, if you bring him, or her, say, to some place like Mercury, to an establishment that seems to be completely at odds with his purpose in being there, will sooner or later get around to asking what the connection is."

He beamed at the man who had spoken.

"Then," Minault went on, "when you give him the answer, it's liable to sink in and promote further thought, instead of merely being filed as a completed explanation. Which is what is likely to happen to it if you just volunteer the information."

There was a general round of smiles.

"All right," said the one who had asked, "any one of us could have been the patsy. And you still haven't answered me."

"Quite right," said Minault. "Well, the point is that human beings react this way because they have an innate curiosity. A machine—call it a technological monster—may have everything else, but it'll be bound to lack innate curiosity. That is a talent reserved for living beings."

He paused again. Nobody said anything.

"Now our world," Minault said, "is at the present time firmly in the grip of a mechanical monster, whose head—if you want to call it that—is the World Engineer's Complex. That monster is opposed to us and can keep all too good a tab on us through every purchase we make with our credit numbers, every time we use the public transportation or eat a meal or rent a place to live—that is, it can as long as we stay on Earth. The Complex of sustaining equipment at Springboard here is officially a part of the Complex-Major back on Earth. But actually there's no connection beyond the bridge of transportation and communication between these two planets." He smiled at the group.

"So," he went on, "we hide here, under the cloak of Springboard. Actually, we control Springboard. But its work is not our work—it merely serves us as a cover. Of course, we're an open secret to those Springboard workers who aren't Chantry Guild members as well. But a machine, as I say, doesn't react as a human being would. If it doesn't see anything, it simply assumes nothing is there—it doesn't poke and pry into dark corners, because it *might* find enemies."

A hand was up. Turning his head slightly, Paul saw it was the cheerful-looking young woman.

"Yes?" said Minault.

"That doesn't make sense," she said. "The World Engineer's Complex is run by men, not machines."

"Ah," said Minault. "But you're making the assumption that the World Engineer and his staff are in control. They aren't. They are controlled by the physics of the society of our time, which in turn is controlled by the Earth Complex—to give it a convenient name—without which that society couldn't exist."

She frowned.

"You mean"—she wavered a moment on the verge of plunging into the cold waters of the wild statement—"the Complex-Major has *intelligence?*"

"Oh, I'm pretty sure we can say that," replied Minault cheerfully. "Fantastic amounts of knowledge, of course; but a sort of definite rudimentary intelligence as well. But I don't think that's what you meant to ask. What you meant to ask was whether the Complex-Major—Super-

door behind Minault, he caught sight of the girl, who had just button-holed the large man.

"I think you're quite wrong about the power of imagination you implied to the Complex-Major," she was saying, severely.

Chapter 13

"You've handled explosives before?" asked the lean instructor with the sun-leathered face above the open collar. He was holding a package of plastic, adhesive blasting jelly with a three-minute pinch fuse.

"Yes," said Paul.

Paul stood on one cliff-edge of a remarkably realistic simulation of a mountain gorge some five hundred feet wide, across which had been thrown the thin long web of a temporary snap-to arch bridge of magnesium-alloy sections. The bridge-end by which Paul and the instructor stood, just the two of them, had been anchored in a local timber cradle, or box, filled with loose rock. And the cradle extended its wooden underarms in support about fifteen feet out from the lip of the cliff.

"This amount of jelly," said the instructor, hefting it, "can be carried inconspicuously in a brief case and still leave room for enough other material to make it look as if the brief case is full. It's powerful enough to cut two or three of those timbers or one or two of the metal members you see there. How would you go about completely knocking out this bridge with it?"

Paul looked again at the bridge. In the past nine days since his first class he had been put through a number of *sessions*—that was the only word to describe them. They appeared to be classes, on a strange variety of subjects, some of which appeared to bear no relation to the Chantry Guild. The longest of them had lasted not much more than twenty minutes, and the information imparted by each of them had been obscure. In fact, it had not been quite clear whether the intent of the sessions had been to inform or to test the journeyman audience, which seemed to consist of different individuals from session to session. Paul was privately of the opinion that the intent had been both to inform and test—and probably, as well, to stimulate and confuse. Some of the journeymen, he was sure, were ringers. Some of the sessions had been nonsense.

And this session—himself alone with the instructor, the explosive, and the simulated bridge in the mountains on Earth. Was it instruction, test, nonsense—or something else?

The simulation was a magnificent job. For the scene it pretended to show was clearly an impossibility, here deep under the surface of Mercury's rocky hide. What Paul's eyes saw was a gorge at least eight hundred feet in depth, up from which came the distant sound of a narrow mountain river in its gallop to lower levels. The air was the thin, dry air of high altitudes. The sky was cloudless.

The question was, How much was real and how much false? For if the blasting-jelly block was real, and it was to be set off in the reality of a small underground room of the size Paul had had his sessions in lately, then it would take Alternate Laws indeed to show cause why Paul and the instructor should survive the explosion. Paul laid his hand on the timber cradle and looked over the cliff edge. His gaze plunged away into spray-misted depths. There was distance down there, by any test of his feelings. Just how much, he could not be sure. But it *felt* deep below the cliff. On the other hand, under his hand the materials of the bridge felt solid but deceitful.

"Well," said Paul, "I'm no expert on bridges. But I imagine the trick would be to break this end loose, so that it falls. If this end goes down, it'll tear the other end loose and it'll all drop into the gorge."

"Good enough," said the instructor. "How'd you go about breaking this end loose?"

"I think," said Paul, pointing to where the end of the cradle met a magnesium I-beam, fifteen feet out above the gorge's depth, "if we blew it loose just there, cutting that stringer, or whatever the proper term is, that runs along the left side of the travel-surface of the bridge, the weight of the rest of it would cause it to sag and twist, and tear the other stringer loose. Then this whole end would drop."

"All right." The instructor handed the block of jelly to Paul. "Let's see you do it."

Paul looked at the bridge again. Then he stuffed the block of jelly inside the waistband of his slacks and began to climb out along the timbers of the cradle. The lack of a second arm hampered him but not so much as Paul thought it might have seemed to the instructor. The strength of his remaining arm was such as to lift the weight of his body from angles clearly impossible to an ordinary climber. When he got to the end of the stone enclosing the timbers, Paul paused, ostensibly to rest, but actually to reach some sort of conclusion.

The bridge still felt deceitful. He quietly loosed a splinter from the timber on which he rested, and dropped it. It floated down until he lost sight of it some thirty or forty feet below. So, that much of distance under him at least was real. He looked once more at the spot where he would stick the explosive.

It was at a point just above the single final timber of the supporting cradle. He would have to stand on that timber and place the jelly above the upright at the timber's end, where that upright met the magnesium I-beam. He began to move again. He climbed on up to the I-beam and out onto it until he was above the timber. Hanging to the I-beam, he cautiously let his feet down until they rested on the timber.

Then, as unobtrusively as possible, he increased his hold on the I-beam and pressed down with both feet on the timber.

There was a sudden screech of tearing wood. The timber ripped away from beneath him, and he dropped suddenly to the length of his arm, and hung there sustained only by his grip on the I-beam. Below him he saw the falling timber on which he would have stood tumbling and shrinking until it vanished suddenly fifty or sixty feet below him. Still hanging, he looked across to the point where the underfoot timber had been joined to the upright by a metal collar held by four thick magnesium rivets.

There were no rivet-hole marks or broken rivet ends

in the wood of the upright at all. What was visible was the snapped end of a quarter-inch-diameter wooden dowel rod.

Paul pulled himself easily back up on the I-beam. The bridge stood firm and secure—it had been balanced, evidently, somewhat differently than it appeared to be, on its supports. He climbed back to the instructor, on solid ground, and handed the jelly block back to the man.

"Now what?" Paul said.

"Well," said the instructor, "we'll go up to the front offices. I don't know what your master will say, and of course it's up to him. But as far as I'm concerned, I'd say you've graduated."

They left the simulated scene in the mountains and went out into the Station proper, and took an elevator up a good number of levels. Paul had the impression that they were almost to, if not right at, the surface. And this impression was justified a second or two later when they entered a large lounge-office with, not a vision tank, but an actual window looking out on the yellow twilight and the witches' garden of Mercury's surface around the Station.

Jase was there, along with Heber, the white-mustached unlisted member, and a couple of men Paul did not recognize. The instructor had Paul wait while he went over and talked to the three for a few minutes in a voice too low for Paul to hear. Then Jase came over alone, and the instructor, with the other two men, went over to one of the desks at the other end of the room and began going over what, judging from their quite audible conversation, were the files of journeymen currently undergoing tests.

"Come on over to the window," said Jase. Paul followed him. The slim, dark young man was as relaxed as Paul had ever seen him, though he still walked with the prowling balance of a cat. "Sit down."

Paul sat, in a low, comfortably overstuffed chair. Jase took one opposite.

"To all intents and purposes," said Jase, and his deep-set, clear brown eyes watched Paul closely, "you're a Chantry Guild member now. Before you first came to me, you'd gotten the psychiatric viewpoint on yourself and your missing arm. Now, I'll tell you the true situation from the point of someone like myself who is acquainted with the Alternate Laws."

He stopped.

"—You were going to say something," he said.

"No," said Paul.

"All right," said Jase, "here it is, then. You have an ability under the Alternate Laws which is probably parapsychological in nature. I told you when I first met you—and I've an ability myself where it comes to judging character—something to the effect that your arrogance was astounding."

Paul frowned. He had all but put aside the memory of the Necromancer calling him arrogant. It was the one thing he could not accept about himself.

"I understand now better why you should be so arrogant," Jase was saying. "I've no idea, none of us have in the regular membership, about the possibilities or limitations of your ability. But we've no doubt about its essential nature. Your ability is to make use of the Alternate Laws for purposes of almost total defense. We've done everything but try to kill you outright and without reservation. You've come through beautifully. Tell me, do you think you could explain to me in words just how you came to suspect that bridge timber just a little while ago? I'm not asking you to explain, I'm asking you if you think you *could* explain it to me."

"No," said Paul, slowly. "No, I don't think so."

"We thought as much. Well, what you want to do with your ability from here on out is up to you. I myself think that the reason a grafted arm won't take on your left side there, is because this defensive ability of yours sees some danger to you in an arm graft. If you find what that danger is, maybe you can discover another counter to it, and the next arm you have attached to you will live instead of dying. But, as I say, that's up to you. However, there's something else."

He stopped. There seemed to be almost a touch of indecision in his manner, for the first time since Paul had met him.

"As I say," said Jase not quite as quickly as he usually

spoke, "in all but name now, you're a member. We haven't only been active with you up here, but we've been active for you back down on Earth. If you go back, you'll have to stand police investigation in connection with the death of Kevin Malorn, that man in the Koh-i-Nor you took the drug to."

"I was wondering about that," said Paul.

"You needn't wonder any longer," said Jase. "The purchase desk in the music section of the library at Chicago Complex Directory now has among its records one showing that you purchased a song tape there at the same time that Malorn was being killed. You will simply have to show up and add your testimony to the evidence of the record. Since the records are machine-made and regarded as untamperable, you'll be clear of any connection with Malorn's death an hour or so after arriving back in Chicago."

"I see." Paul nodded. "The song tape—it isn't one of Kantele singing something about *'in apple comfort time,'* is it?"

Jase frowned.

"Yes," he said. "As a matter of fact it is. Why?"

"Nothing," said Paul. "I've heard it, but not all the way through."

"It's a natural choice," said Jase. "The record shows my credit number—you were buying it at my request. That's reasonable enough, since Kantele and I are old friends and the song was written for her by Blunt."

"Blunt?"

"Why yes." Jase smiled a little at him. "You didn't know the Guildmaster wrote music?"

"No."

"He does a great many things," said Jase, a little dryly. "However, the point is you can go back to Earth as free as you ever were. Except that as a Guild member you'll be required to take orders from the masters, like myself."

"I see," said Paul, a little grimly.

"Do you?" replied Jase. He sighed. "I don't think you do. Not by a damn sight. Would you listen with an open mind for about five minutes?"

"Of course," said Paul.

"All right," said Jase. "Modern man got his motor to turning over with the Renaissance. At that time two things were initiated. One was the attitude of enlightened inquiry that began people on the road to a technological society and civilization. The road that sought to build a man a home and keep him well fed and happy within it by use of the machine."

"Which was bad?" said Paul.

"No, no," said Jase. "There's nothing wrong with a prosthetic appliance if nothing else is available. But you'd rather have a flesh-and-blood arm just like your own grafted on, wouldn't you?"

"Go on," said Paul.

"However, the original role of the machine started to get perverted around the time of the industrial revolution. It came to be regarded not as a means to a desired end, but as part of the end in itself. The process accelerated in the nineteenth century, and exploded in the twentieth. Man kept demanding more in the way of service from his technology, and the technology kept giving it—but always at the price of a little more of man's individual self-contained powers. In the end—in our time —our technology has become second thing to a religion. Now we're trapped in it. And we're so enfeebled by our entrapment that we tell ourselves it's the only possible way to live. That no other way exists."

"I——" began Paul, and checked himself.

"Yes, 'I,' " said Jase. "The arrogant 'I,' with the built-in survival qualities. But other people aren't like you."

"That wasn't what I was going to say," observed Paul.

"It doesn't matter," said Jase. "The point isn't you, but the world, which is at the mercy of an ever-growing technological system."

"Which the Chantry Guild wishes to attack."

"Attack?" said Jase. "The Chantry Guild was formed by Walt Blunt to protect its members against the attack of the technological system."

"What you're saying," Paul said, "is that your members grew up out of something other than the technological system."

"That's quite right," said Jase calmly. "They did. And so did you."

Paul looked searchingly at the Necromancer, but the dark face was as full of honesty as Paul had ever seen it.

"I said, two things were initiated at the time of the Renaissance," said Jase. "One was the roots of the single system that has given us our technological civilization, that says there is only one way for Man to live, and that's swaddled by the machine. And the other was all other systems—the principle of freedom which lies at the base of the Alternate Laws. The first would make Man an inferior, the second acknowledges his superiority."

He looked at Paul as if expecting a protest.

"I'm not in disagreement with the idea of superiority," said Paul.

"Side by side, but not noticed except by a few," said Jase, "while everybody and his Uncle Charlie was engaged in making a god out of the machine, a few talented people were proving that Man had already reached that level of deity and wasn't even started yet. Genius was at work in every generation—and genius works with the Alternate Laws. Only, after a while the machine got enough muscles so that it started crowding genius—and that brings it down to our time, Paul."

"We do seem to end there, all the time," said Paul, and could not stop himself from smiling a little.

"I thought you promised me an open mind," said Jase.

"I'm sorry."

"All right, then," said Jase. "Answer me something. Suppose you're a person in any generation up to about fifty years ago whose abilities and inclinations make him inclined to have something more or something different than what's available to the mass of people in his time. What happens?"

"I'm listening," said Paul, "with an open mind."

"He can go under to the general attitude and be essentially destroyed by denying his own possibilities. Or he can rise above the general attitude and keep afloat by sheer dint of extra ability-muscle. Agreed?"

Paul nodded.

"In other words, he can lose or win his own personal battle with the mass-opinion of his time. In either case he's resolved his problem." Jase looked at Paul. Paul nodded again.

"But in our time," said Jase, "such a person isn't up against the opinions and attitudes of his fellows. He's up against an attitude brought to life and resolved into a mechanical monster that can't be reasoned with, and can't be adjusted to. He can't win for the same reason he can't outwrestle a bulldozer with his bare hands. And he can't submit because the bulldozer doesn't understand submission. It only understands a complete job."

Jase leaned forward with his hands on both of his knees. The emotion in the man came at Paul as sharp as an arrow.

"Don't you understand?" asked the Necromancer. "The Chantry Guild was established because the technological system of our own time was trying to kill these people who belong to the Guild—each and every one of them, and any more like them—kill them off." His eyes blazed at Paul. "Just as it's been trying to kill you!"

Paul looked back at him for a long moment.

"Me?" he asked, at last.

"The weather warning you didn't get when you were out sailing," said Jase. "The temporal disorientation that caused you to be caught by the starting ore cars in the shaft of the mine. The misdirection of the subway car that stranded you in the middle of a street cleared for use by a marching society. Yes," he added, as Paul's eyebrows raised slightly, "we had a tracer on you from the time you first left my place. That's usual." He looked a little thin-lipped for a moment. "It's part of the war between us and it."

"I see," said Paul, his mind running back over a number of things.

"You're in it, on the side of the Guild, whether you like it or not. We'd like your active, working co-operation. If your ability under the Alternate Laws is what it seems to be, you'll be more valuable to your fellow Guild members than anyone else could be."

"Why?" asked Paul.

Jase shrugged a little angrily.

"I won't tell you that—*now*, of course," he said. "How could I? You've got to commit yourself to the Guild—that is, try for the rank of Necromancer, a master in the Guild. We'll put you to the test. If you come through all right, then some time in the future you'll learn what you can do for the Guild. You'll hear it from the only man who can give you commands once you're a master —the Guildmaster himself, Walt Blunt."

"Blunt!"

Paul felt the name slide into place with the events here on Mercury at Springboard. He felt a rage of passion remembered, and a lonely sorrow, and then the hard, driving core of his determination to bring this man Blunt face to face.

"Of course," Jase was saying. "Who else could there be to give orders to the master rank? Blunt's our general."

"I'm committed," said Paul, quietly. "What do I do?"

"Well," said Jase, taking his hands off his knees and sitting up straight, "I told you it's this ability of yours we want to determine. I said we'd done everything but try to kill you outright and without reservation. We'd like to take that last step now—make a serious effort with the resources of the Guild behind it and no safety hatch—and see if you survive."

Chapter 14

Master and Necromancer in name only, and under the shadow of a sometime attempt to be made upon his life, Paul returned to Earth and the Chicago Complex—ostensibly from a canoe trip up in the Quetico-Superior wilderness park area along the Canadian border near Lake Superior. He was picked up at the Complex Outer Terminal, taken to Complex Police Headquarters, and gave his statement concerning his whereabouts at the time of Malorn's murder by person or persons unknown. A police-beat reporter for one of the newssheets questioned him perfunctorily as he was leaving after his release by the police.

"How does it feel?" asked the reporter, matching strides with Paul as Paul walked toward the waiting cars at the Police terminal, "not to be facing a possible sentence of death?"

"You tell me," said Paul, as he got in a two-man car and went off. The reporter considered a moment and erased the reply from his hand recorder. It had been too flippant, he thought.

"'I am relieved, of course,'" dictated the reporter into the recorder. "'However, knowing modern police methods and equipment I never had any real doubt they would find out I hadn't done it.'" He put the recorder back in his pocket and returned to the booking desk inside.

Paul, reporting to Jase, who also had returned, was told to rent himself an apartment not too far from Suntden Place and amuse himself for the present. Paul did so. There followed several weeks of idleness in which Paul slept late, wandered around the Complex soaking up the feel of it and its crowds, and generally waited for his personal ax to fall.

It did not fall. Paul seemed almost forgotten—pensioned off and put aside by the Chantry Guild. Yet Jase, when Paul checked in with the Necromancer, and Kantele, on the one or two brief glimpses Paul had of her, seemed caught up in a smoothly constant, high-temperature state of activity. On one of his visits Paul had attempted to find out how he might get in touch with Blunt. Jase had told him quite bluntly that when Paul needed to know such information, it would be given to him. Blunt, Paul gathered, had no fixed address. His location at any time was a matter for his own immediate decision, and known only to those like Jase and Kantele, who were close to him.

The first week in May, on a Monday, found Paul up around the Wisconsin Dells, ostensibly squirrel-hunting. He had largely given over any conscious watch for the attack he had been promised by Jase, but that anterior part of his mind which took care of such things had not forgotten. Midday found him seated with his back to the trunk of a silver maple, half drowsy with the warmth of the strong spring sun out of a blue sky, and lost in a collection of newspapers and periodicals. However, his gun was across his knees, a steep fifty-foot cliff of loose gravel fell away behind the maple, and before him he could see clear down through a small grove of maple, pine, and poplar to a wide field of black earth faintly dusted with the new green of coming corn plants. It was an automatically perfect defensive position.

There were gray squirrels in the trees down the slope. They had taken care not to get too close when Paul had first settled himself against the trunk of the maple, but, *Sciurus carolinensis* not being known for any lack of curiosity, they had been allowing themselves to work and play closer to where he sat in motionlessness. Now, after about two hours of Paul's sitting and reading, one slim youngster had grown so swashbuckling as to slip out from behind a narrow poplar trunk not fifteen feet from the human and sit up boldly to stare.

Paul was aware of these small attentions, but he felt a certain definite pleasure in letting them go on uninterrupted. The last thing from his mind was the desire to kill. He had more than a moral conviction against it, he was discovering. He almost regarded it as a sort of self-performed amputation. Particularly at this moment when he had allowed himself to go deep into the life and stir of the small section of the world at the moment around him. He let himself float in the sensation of the warming earth, the light and movement surrounding, and gave the full attention of his thinking processes to the reading material he had brought with him.

The material was merely a chance selection among the many publications currently on sale or merely available for the picking up. But they struck hard upon him. He found himself wondering how, with such a universal voice of unhappiness sounding in the world, he had failed to be overwhelmed by it before.

The publications were full of the statistics of distress. Testing of grade-school children revealed that seven per cent of those under the age of eight were headed for major mental illnesses. The world crime rate had been climbing steadily for fifty years and this last year had jumped twenty-three per cent again. And this in a world in which nobody needed to lack for the necessities, and even most of the luxuries, of life. The world suicide rate was climbing sharply. Cultism was commonplace. Hysteria such as the marching societies exemplified was growing steadily. The birth rate was down.

Article after article either explored the situation, or offered some self-help method of individual adjustment to it. And yet—Paul went back through the pages before him again—there was enough of other topics, of sports, news, humor, art, and science, so that someone like himself who had not suffered individually could ignore the notes of trouble in the general symphony of modern achievement otherwise.

And still—Paul frowned a little. He did not believe what he read, or what people told him. He believed only what he himself could check against the touchstone of his feelings, and it occurred to him now that he seemed to sense something about the catalogue of unhappinesses. A faint tone as of something whining. Or was he being unfair?

He pushed the newssheets and periodicals aside, and half-closed his eyes to the sunlight coming through the young leaves. He was conscious of the weight of the gun across his legs as well as the peaceful rustlings of the woods. The adventurous squirrel had been followed into the open by two of his fellows, but the first one, the one with guts, was still in the lead. As Paul watched without stirring, the adventurous one made a sudden dash right up to the toe of Paul's left hiking boot, and examined it with a quivering black nose.

The other two followed after. Man, thought Paul slowly, proceeds by dashes like the squirrel, and each new discovery is the one which is going to turn the world upside down. Each new setback seems to threaten eternal night. He looked at the squirrels. All three were now examining the rifle-stock of the gun where it projected out into the air beyond his right knee on a level with their small, black, fascinated eyes. He tried to feel what it was like to be one with them, and for a second his point of view flooded into a fantastic, pillared world of attack and defense, sleep, hunger, and the unknown.

Another squirrel raced suddenly toward him from the cover of the nearest tree. Suddenly there was concerted movement. As the newcomer reached the two followers, all three with unnaturally perfect teamwork threw their squirrel-weights suddenly against and on top of the projecting rifle stock. The gun tilted and swung, the muzzle of the barrel coming up thump against the left side of Paul's chest.

And at the same moment the adventurous squirrel leaped fair and true for the trigger button of the gun.

All in one explosive instant, it happened. And all in one movement of coldly swift and certain reaction, Paul's arm had galvanized into movement with the first rush of the fourth squirrel across the dappled earth. His long fingers met the leaping squirrel in mid-air, caught him, and broke his neck.

There was a scuttling rush away in all directions. Then silence. Paul found himself standing on his feet with the spilled gun, the scattered throwaway publications at his feet, and no other living creature in sight. He held the dead squirrel still in his hand.

Paul's heart thumped once, savagely, in his chest. He looked down at the dead squirrel. The small, black, animal eyes were squeezed tightly shut, as they might have been in any living being forced into risking all, in one wild tourney with the unknown.

The wound of an amputation bled somewhere in the depths of Paul. His eyes dimmed. The sun had lost its way momentarily behind a cloud, and the forest floor was all one color. Paul laid the small gray body gently down at the foot of the silver maple and smoothed its rumpled fur. He picked up his gun by the cold, slickly-machined metal of its barrel, and went off through the trees.

When he got back to his apartment in the Chicago Complex, Jase was already inside it and waiting for him as he entered.

"Congratulations," said Jase, "—Necromancer."

Paul looked at him. Involuntarily, Jase stepped back.

Chapter 15

Paul was, he learned in the next few days, now a part of the more or less "Cabinet" group in the Guild, which operated directly with and under Blunt himself. The other Cabinet members consisted of Jase, Kantele, Burton McLeod—the heavy broadsword of a man Paul had met earlier in Jase's apartment—and an elusive gray wafer of a little man whose name was Eaton White. White, it seemed, was posted high on the personal staff of Kirk Tyne, and the first thing he did was take Paul in to see Tyne about a job in the World Engineer's office.

"I suppose," asked Tyne, when he had shaken hands with Paul in the clear morning sunlight coming through the high windows of a luxurious office lounge two hundred levels above the Chicago traffic, "you wonder why I seem so little hesitant to have a member of the Guild on my personal staff? Sit down, sit down. You, too, Eat."

Paul and Eaton White took comfortable chairs. Tyne also sat down, stretching his slim legs before him. He looked as fit as a well-kept bowstring, and as unfrayed by the demands of his work. His eyes, glancing directly into Paul's under neat brown eyebrows, were startlingly perceptive.

"I was a little surprised, yes," said Paul.

"Well, there's a number of reasons," said Tyne. "Did you ever consider the difficulties of changing the present?"

"Changing the present?"

"It's impossible," said Tyne, almost merrily. "Though very few people stop to think about it and realize the fact. When you pick up an inch of the present to move it, you also pick up several thousand miles of history."

"I see," said Paul. "You mean, to change the present you'd have to first change the past."

"Exactly," replied Tyne. "And that's what reformers invariably forget. They talk about changing the future. As if doing so was some new and great feat. Nonsense.

Our main business as living human beings is changing the future. In fact, that's all we can change. The present is the result of the past; and even if we could monkey with the past, who'd dare to? Change one tiny factor and the result in the present might well be the whole human race blown apart. So your reformers, your great changers, are kidding themselves. They talk about changing the future, when what they really mean is that they want to change the present, the present they're living in right at the moment. They don't realize they're trying to move furniture that's already nailed down."

"So you think the Chantry Guild is made up of furniture movers?" asked Paul.

"Essentially—essentially," said Tyne. He sat forward in his chair. "Oh, I want you to know I have a high opinion of the Guild, and the Guild members. And I have something more than a high opinion of Walt Blunt. Walt awes me, and I don't mind admitting it. But that doesn't alter the fact that he's barking up the wrong tree."

"Apparently," said Paul, "he thinks the same of you."

"Of course!" said Tyne. "He'd be bound to. He's a natural revolutionist. I'm a real revolutionist. I know the present can't be changed, so I concentrate on changing the future. Really changing it—by hard work, discovery, and progress; the way it actually gets changed."

Paul looked at him interestedly.

"What's your idea of the future?" asked Paul.

"Utopia," said Tyne. "A practical utopia that we've all adjusted to. That's all that's really wrong with the present, you know. We've achieved, through our science and technology, a practical utopia. Our only trouble is that we aren't adjusted to it yet. We keep feeling there must be a catch somewhere, something to be fought against and licked. That's Walt's trouble, incidentally. He can't help feeling he ought to be revolting against something intolerable. And since he can't find anything intolerable, he's gone to a great deal of trouble to work up a revolt against what's not only tolerable, but infinitely desirable —the very things we've been working for for centuries. Comfort, freedom, and wealth."

"I take it," said Paul, and frowned for a second as

the ghost of a small gray squirrel scampered for a moment unbidden across his thoughts, "you don't worry too much about the increases in crime, suicides, mental disorders, and so forth?"

"I consider them. I don't *worry* about them," said Tyne, leaning forward with argumentative relish. "In the Super-Complex—I mean by that, the reconciling units here in the Headquarters building—we've got the greatest tool ever forged by Man for solving all Man's problems. It'll take a few generations, no doubt, but eventually we'll iron out the essentially emotional reaction that's causing these things you talk about."

"Emotional reaction?" asked Paul.

"Of course! For the first time in the history of Man, for the first time since he first stuck his nose out of a nice safe hole in the ground, people have absolutely nothing to be afraid of, nothing to worry about. Is it any wonder that all their little individual quirks and idiosyncrasies, sprout wings and fly off with them?"

"I can't believe," said Paul slowly, "that the causes for what I read about in the newssheets and periodicals now are caused just by idiosyncrasies in the individual."

"Well, of course, it isn't that simple." Tyne sat back in his chair. "There are strong group elements in the human character. Religion, for one—that's at the root of all these sects and cults. The tendency toward hysteria and mob action that's been the cause of the marching societies. We're getting a social fragmentation. But just because Utopia's new, and there's no reason not to run hog wild. As I say, a generation or two will see us settling back down."

He stopped talking.

"Well," said Paul, when it seemed to be up to him, "this is all very interesting. I take it you're trying to convert me."

"Exactly right," said Tyne. "As I say, I don't agree with Walt, but he recruits some of the best material in the world. Eaton here's an example. And poor Malorn was a Guild member."

"Malorn!" said Paul, looking closely at the World Engineer.

"Yes—in a way you might say I owe you something

for having been unfairly accused in connection with his death. It was a breakdown misfunction in the police machinery, and I'm responsible for the smooth working of all machinery."

"But that isn't why you'd give me a job?"

"Not by itself, of course. No. But Eat here speaks highly of you and says you don't seem to be completely blinkered and blinded by all those theories of Walt's. I'm willing to take a chance on talking you over to my point of view, if you're willing to take the chance of being talked. And of course, Walt will be tickled to have you on the inside, here. You see, he thinks he's outsmarting me by being completely open and aboveboard about planting his people on me."

"And you," said Paul, "think you're outsmarting him."

"I know I am," said Tyne, smiling. "I have an intelligent friend who tells me so."

"It seems to be settled, then," said Paul. He stood up. Tyne and Eaton rose with him. "I'd like to meet your intelligent friend, sometime."

"Some day, you might do that," said Tyne. They shook hands. "In fact, I imagine you will. It was this friend's recommendation that rather clinched this matter of taking you on here."

Paul looked at the World Engineer sharply. With his last words something had come and gone so swiftly in the other man that it was impossible now to say what it might have been. It was as if a metal edge had shown itself for a moment.

"I'll look forward to it, then," said Paul. And Eaton led him out.

Outside the World Engineer Complex Headquarters they parted. Eaton went back in to work. Paul went on to Jase's.

As he stepped through the entrance to Jase's apartment and put his key back in his pocket, he heard voices. One was Jase's. But the other—he stopped at the sound of it—was the deep, resonant, and sardonic voice of Blunt.

"I realize, Jase," the voice of Blunt was saying, "that you find me a little too much of a playboy at times. It's something you'll just have to bear with, however."

"I don't mean that at all, Walt!" The younger man'
voice was charged and grim. "Who's going to lay down
rules for *you,* of all people? It's just that if I find myself
having to take over, I want to know what you had in
mind."

"If you take over, it's your own mind you'll follow
and that's the way it should be," said Blunt. "Let's cross
such bridges when we come to them. You may not
have to take over. Who just came in?"

The last words coincided with Paul's stepping around
the corner from the entrance hall into the main lounge
of Jase's apartment. The wall entrance to the office in
Kantele's apartment next door was open, and through it
Paul now saw the wide shoulders and back of Blunt,
with the dark, startled visage of Jase beyond.

"Me. Formain," answered Paul, and he walked toward
the office. But Jase stepped swiftly past Blunt and came
down into his own lounge, closing the office entrance behind him.

"What is it?" asked Jase.

"It seems I'm now on the immediate staff of the World
Engineer," said Paul. He looked past Jase at the closed
wall. "That's Walter Blunt in there, isn't it? I'd like to
speak to him."

He stepped around Jase, went to the wall, and opened
it. Within, the office was empty. He turned back to Jase.

"Where did he go?"

"I imagine," said Jase, dryly, "if he'd wanted to stay
and talk to you, he'd have stayed."

Paul turned again and went on into the office. He went
through it into the farther reaches of Kantele's apartment. It was a feminine dwelling, but empty. Paul
paused by its front door, but there was no clue about it
to signal whether Walter Blunt had walked out through it
in the last few minutes.

He went back to the office, and through it. Jase was
no longer in his own lounge. He seemed to have left the
apartment. Paul was about to leave, too, in a mood of
puzzled disturbance, when the entrance to Jase's apartment clicked open—he heard it—and someone came
in.

Expecting Jase, Blunt, or both, he was turning toward the entrance hall when Kantele came out of it, carrying some sort of package, and stopped.

"Paul!" she said.

It was not a happy, or even pleased, sounding of his name. Rather, it was on a note of dismay that she said it.

"Yes," he said, a little sadly.

"Where's"—she hesitated—"Jase?"

"And Walter Blunt," he said. "I'd like to know where they disappeared to, and why, myself."

"They probably had to go someplace." She was ill-at-ease. It showed in the way she held the package to her.

"I hadn't realized," he said, reaching for a neutral topic, "that Blunt wrote that 'apple comfort' song of yours. Jase told me."

She looked abruptly a little sharply at him. Almost challengingly.

"That surprised you, did it?" she asked.

"Why——" he said. "No."

"It didn't?"

"I don't know," he said, "exactly whether to call it 'surprise.' I didn't know the Guildmaster wrote songs, that was all. And——" He stopped, feeling her bristle.

"And what?"

"Nothing," he said, as peaceably as he could, "I only heard the first verse before you came in that day, and the one time I heard it before. But it seemed to me more a young man's song."

She strode angrily past him. He got the impression that she was rather pleased than otherwise to find something to get angry about. She punched buttons on Jase's music player and swung about with her back to it.

"Then it's time you heard the second verse, isn't it?" she asked. A second later her own voice swelled from the player behind her.

> *In apple comfort, long I waited thee*
> *And long I thee in apple comfort waited.*

"Young man's song," she said bitingly.

> *In lonely autumn and uncertain springtime*
> *My apple longing for thee was not sated.*

The clear, mountain rivulet of her recorded voice paused, and then went on into the second verse. She looked across at him with her eyes fixed and her lips together.

> *Now come thee near anigh my autumn winding.*
> *In cider-stouted jugs, my memories*
> *Shall guard thee by the fireside of my passion,*
> *And at my life's end keep thy gentle lees.*

The music shut off. He saw that she was profoundly moved by it and deeply unhappy. He went to her.

"I'm sorry," he said, standing before her. "You mustn't let what I think disturb you. Forget I had any opinion at all."

She tried to take a step back from him and found the wall behind her. She leaned her head back against the wall, and he put out his long hand to the wall beside her, half-convinced for a moment that she was about to fall. But she stood with her shoulders against the wall and closed her eyes, turning her face away to one side. Tears squeezed from under her closed eyelids and ran down her cheeks.

"Oh," she whispered, "why won't you leave me alone?" She pressed her face against the wall. "Please, just leave me alone!"

Torn by her unhappiness, he turned and left, leaving her still standing there, pressed in sorrow against the wall.

Chapter 16

In the days that followed, Paul did not see her again. It was more than obvious that she was avoiding him, and she must at least have spoken to Jase about him, for the Necromancer made it a point one day to speak about her.

"You're wasting your time, there," Jase said bluntly. "She's Walt's."

"I know that," said Paul. He glanced across the table at Jase. The other man had met him for lunch near World Engineering Headquarters, bringing him a long and curious list of cults and societies with which, as Jase put it, the Guild had some "influence." Paul was supposed to learn the names and habits of these groups against some future date when the Guild might want to cultivate them. Paul accepted the list without protest. In spite of the fact that he was theoretically supposed to take orders only from the Guildmaster, he had yet to meet Blunt. Jase brought him all his instructions. Paul had decided not to make an issue of this for the moment. There was too much to be learned even as things were.

There were about sixty thousand members in the Chantry Guild. Of these, perhaps fifteen hundred had dramatic parapsychological talents. Even in a world which accepted such things—even though mostly as interesting parlor tricks or talents on a par with wiggling one's ears —fifteen hundred people represented a pretty remarkable pool of potential ability. Paul was supposed to learn all about each one of the fifteen hundred odd: who could do what, and when, and, most important, who was improving his powers by exploring them in the curious, mystical, long-way-around light of the Alternate Laws.

In addition, there were other aspects of the Guild for Paul to learn, like the list Jase had just brought over on Paul's lunch hour. And all the work connected with the World Engineering Complex, where Tyne had Paul studying procedure like any executive trainee.

Weather all over the world had been freakishly bad. In the southern hemisphere the winter had been stormy and cold. Here, the summer days were muggy and sweltering, but no rain fell. The Weather Control Complex found itself in the position of having to rob Peter to pay Paul—moisture diverted to one needy section of the Earth left other sections either twice as arid or drowned in torrential, flooding rains that caused widespread damage. It was no crisis, but it was annoyingly uncomfortable. The internal climate of the great city Com-

plexes held the outside weather at arms length, but the
emotional impact of the season's aberrancies came
through even into air-conditioned interiors like this one
where Paul and Jase sat at lunch.

"It's just as well you realize she does belong to Walt,"
said Jase. For perhaps the first time since Paul had met
him, there was a gentleness in Jase's voice. "She's Finnish, you know—you know where her name comes from?"

"No," said Paul. "No, I don't."

"The Kalevala—the Finnish national epic. Longfellow
wrote his Hiawatha poem from it."

"No," said Paul, "I didn't know."

"Kaleva—Finland," said Jase.

(Wind across snow fields. Tinkling among the icicles of
a cavern—I knew it the first time, thought Paul.)

"Kaleva had three sons. Handsome Lemminkainen,
the art-smith, Ilmarinen, and the ancient Väinämöinen."
Paul watched Jase with interest; for the first time the
drive and rush of the man was gone. He spoke the names
of the old legend with the lingering love of a scholar in
his voice. "Väinämöinen invented the sacred harp—
Kantele. And she is a harp, our Kantele. A harp for the
hand of gods or heroes. That's why Walt holds her, old
as he is, unyielding as he is to anything but his own way
of doing things." Jase shook his head across the table.
"You may be arrogant, Paul. But even you have to face
the fact that Walt's something more than us ordinary
men."

Paul smiled a little. Jase, watching him, laughed shortly. Abruptly the Necromancer was his own hard, glit-
tering self again.

"Because you don't think you can be killed," said Jase,
"you think you can't be defeated, either!"

Paul shook his head.

"I'm quite sure I can be killed," he answered. "It's
the defeat I doubt."

"Why?" asked Jase, leaning forward. Paul was a little
surprised to see that the man was seriously asking.

"I don't know. I—feel it," said Paul, hesitantly.

Jase let the breath out through his nose with a faint,
impatient sound. He stood up.

"Learn that list," he said. "Burt said to tell you he'd

pick you up tonight after you're through at your office, if you weren't otherwise tied up. You might give him a call."

"I will," said Paul, and watched the other man leave, moving lithely and swiftly among the tables of the restaurant.

Burton McLeod, two-handed broadsword with human brain and soul, had become the nearest thing to a close friend Paul could ever remember having in his life. And this just in the past few weeks and months.

McLeod was in his early forties. Occasionally he looked immeasurably older. Sometimes he looked almost boyish. There was a deep, unvarying sadness in him, which was there as a result of the violence he had done, but not as a result of the ordinary reactions.

He did not regret the killing he had done. His conscience saw no reason why any enemy should not die. But deep within him, it saddened him that battle was not sanctified. Surely there had been something right and holy at one time about a flat field, a fair fight, and a fair death? He would never have thought to ask quarter for himself, and it embarrassed him that the world in which he lived insisted upon the concept of unvarying quarter for all, even for those he regarded as needing killing. He was a kind and gentle man, a little shy with those of the human race he considered worthwhile, in which class, along with Blunt, Kantele, and Jase, Paul was pleased and embarrassed in turn to find himself numbered. His mind was brilliant and he was an instinctive bookworm, and his essential moral code was so innate that there seemed to be a wall between him and any possibility of dishonesty.

Like Paul, his life had been solitary. That might have been part of what drew them together. But a mutual honesty and a lack of ordinary fear played a part, also. It began with Paul being sent for some rudimentary tutoring in unarmed self-defense, as part of his Guild teachings, and went on from there with Paul's and McLeod's mutual discovery that Paul's overdeveloped arm was not amenable to ordinary training, or susceptible to ordinary attack and disablement.

"It's speed that does it," McLeod had said, one evening in a gym, after several unsuccessful attempts on his part to lock and hold Paul's arm. "Given speed and leverage, you don't need much in the way of muscle. But you've got the muscle, too." He examined Paul's arm with interest. "I don't understand it. You ought to be slow as a truck. But you're as fast or faster than I am."

"A freak," said Paul, opening and closing his fist to watch the muscles in his forearm bulge and retreat.

"That's it," agreed McLeod, without any overtone of comment. "That isn't just an overdeveloped arm. It's just a properly developed, trained arm for somebody six inches bigger than you. Someone rather lean, but in top shape, and about six-seven or so. Was your other arm as long as this one?"

Paul dropped his arm down by his side. To his intense and sudden interest, he saw that the tips of his fingers hung down almost to his kneecap.

"No," he said. "This one wasn't, either."

"Well," said McLeod, shrugging. He began to put on the shirt he had taken off to instruct Paul. "We didn't really work up a sweat. I'll wait until I get home to shower. Buy you a drink?"

"If I can buy the second," said Paul. And that was the beginning of their friendship.

It was late July of the summer that Jase made his call, left the list of the cults and societies for Paul to learn, and the word about McLeod seeing Paul after working hours that evening.

Paul called up the other man from back at the office and agreed to meet McLeod in the bar of the same restaurant where he had had lunch with Jase. He spent the rest of the afternoon *running the charts,* as the office phrase was, down in the heart of the huge two-hundred-level building that was the core of the world's machinery, actually in the Super-Complex, itself.

This duty was one which everyone on Tyne's staff, including Tyne, had to perform for himself about once a month. The equipment of the Super-Complex was semi-self-adapting. Changes were constantly being made in it to keep it in line with changes being made in the ultimate mechanisms out in the world with which it was in contact and control. Also, within certain limits, it was capable—and exercised that capability—of making changes in itself. Accordingly, everyone on Tyne's staff had the obligation of keeping up their own portfolio of charts and information about the Super-Complex. You started out with a thick sheaf of notices of alteration, and went down among the working levels, checking the actual changes and seeing they were entered in your portfolio. Without these, there might have been a number of shifts in responsibility from one recording, computing, or controlling element to another, and the human staff might have found itself trying to initiate changes through automatic channels that had already been closed.

It was simply the homework connected with the job of being on the World Engineer's staff, the necessary duty of keeping up-to-date in your own field of endeavor.

Nonetheless, in Paul's case he found it to be much more than the routine duty it was supposed to be. Moving about through chance corridors allowed by the mobile units of the Super-Complex itself, surrounded level by level by the impossible intricacies of softly humming and clicking equipment, Paul could now understand why someone like the weak, drug-fogged Malorn could have been pushed over the unstable border of his mind by moving around here. There was life, all right, in this steadily operating maze of understanding and control; Paul felt it certainly and surely. But it was not life in the human sense of the living, and it did not face him directly. Rather, it slid behind the massed equipment, hid in a corridor closed a second before by a unit moving to block a path that had once been open.

The two previous times he had been down to bring his portfolio up to date he had not seemed to notice so much purposefulness to the feeling of mechanical life about him. He wondered if he was becoming sensitized, perhaps in the same way that Malorn had.

The idea was ridiculous. The moment he held Malorn's broken personality up alongside his own for purposes of comparison, that much became immediately plain. Malorn had been afraid.

Paul stood still for a moment on the sixty-seventh level, looking about him. Far down the open corridor in which he was standing, a tall gleaming bank of units slid across the opening, blocking it, and a new path opened up, angling off to the right. It was like being down in among the moving parts of some engine. An engine equipped to be careful of crushing any small creature climbing about within it as it moved to break old connections between its parts, and make new connections.

Paul turned back to his portfolio with a suddenly inquiring eye. It had not occurred to him before to consider areas within the levels of equipment. He, like all other staff members, simply went to the point where it was necessary to check on a change, checked on it, then took the most direct route to the next closest change point. But the portfolio was simply a history of changes running back to the general chart put out at the beginning of each year. He glanced through it.

The forty-ninth to the fifty-second level, he saw, showed no changes whatsoever since the beginning of the year. In this area the chart showed the Earth terminal of the no-time connection with Station Springboard on Mercury, and the equipment dealing with the relationship of this project to Earthside economy, social factors, and science. Paul frowned over the immediate chart of that area. It seemed incredible that an area dealing with research and discovery should have failed to show a multitude of changes in seven months, let alone showing none.

It occurred to Paul, abruptly, that information about the changes in that area might be restricted to certain qualified people. Perhaps to Tyne himself. The World Engineer had, not once but a number of times in the past weeks, recommended that Paul ask about anything that puzzled him. Paul lifted his wrist phone and buzzed the office on the two hundredth level.

"Nancy," he said to the receptionist, "this is Paul. Do you know anything about any area down here I'm not supposed to go into or know about?"

"Why, no," said the girl. In the small tank of Paul's wrist phone, her face was slim, cheerful, but puzzled. "Staff members from this office can go anywhere in the Supe."

"I see," said Paul. "Could I talk to Mr. Tyne?"

"Oh, he just went down into the Supe himself, about five minutes ago."

"Portfolio?"

"That's right."

"He's wearing a phone, isn't he?"

"Just a minute." She glanced at her board. "I guess he must have left it on his desk here. You know he doesn't like wearing one." She grinned at Paul. "It's just the rest of us have to follow rules."

"Well," said Paul, "I'll catch him later after he's back."

"I'll tell him you called, Paul. 'By."

"'By, Nancy." Paul clicked off his phone. He thought for a second and then headed himself for the unchanged area between the forty-ninth and fifty-second levels.

He found it no different on the forty-ninth level than on other levels in the Supe, until he came suddenly upon the long, looming roundness of the three-step accelerator tube. He passed around the end of this and found himself crossing the small open area that was a counterpart of the contact point he had seen at Springboard. This was one end of the no-time pathway that abolished the distance between terminals.

As his first step came down on the highly polished surface of the area, the alarm of a sudden warning rang loudly in his inner sensitivity. He almost checked himself. But just at that moment something attracted his attention otherwise.

The sound of a conversation came to his ears. Both voices used the deeper, male register of tones, and one was the voice of Kirk Tyne. The other voice was unnatural.

They reached Paul's ears down an angled corridor between high units of equipment. Paul went quickly and, he did not think why, quietly up the corridor toward them.

He turned the angle of the corridor. And stopped, finding himself shielded behind the angle of a projecting unit some eighteen or twenty feet high. Just beyond this angle he looked out into a fairly good-sized open space, almost a square, surrounded by units a good two levels in height. Their lower levels were lighted for the benefit of those living people who might need to work among them, as all units were lighted. But their upper part projected up into the dusk where lights were not. All around the square of open space they loomed like finely machined and polished idols in a temple. Tiny below them, facing one wall of these great shapes, stood Tyne.

"There's no doubt about it," Tyne was saying, "the weather—all this rioting and upset. The world situation is abnormal."

"It has been recorded." The voice came from somewhere in the wall of units facing the World Engineer. "It has been symbolized and integrated with the base situation. No apparent need for extraordinary measures is now indicated."

"There's an atmosphere of unrest. I can feel it myself."

"No concrete indications have been signalized or recorded."

"I don't know," said Tyne, almost to himself. He raised his voice slightly. "I think I may override you on this."

"Override," said the voice, "would introduce an uncalculable factor rising to a peak unit influence of twelve per cent and extending over an eighteen-month period."

"I can't simply ignore the situation."

"No situation is ignored. Ordinary measures are in process to correct the aberrancies."

"And you think they'll prove sufficient?"

"They will correct."

"By which you mean, you think they'll correct," said Tyne, a little harshly. "Sometime I'm going to take a summer off and design an honest element of self-doubt for you."

The other voice did not answer.

"What should I do?" asked Tyne, finally.

"Continue normal routine."

"I guess," said Tyne. He turned suddenly and strode off toward an opposite side of the square. Before him, a corridor opened up. He went away down it, and it closed behind him.

Paul was left watching in silence.

Quietly, he came out into the square and looked about him. The units he looked at were in appearance no different than the larger computer elements on other levels.

He walked over to the side where Tyne had stood. But he could not even discern a loud-speaker element in the faces of the units he was observing.

A slight sound behind him made him glance over his shoulder. He turned completely around. The corridor by which he had come to this spot was now closed. The units stood looming, side by side, unbroken around him.

"Paul Formain," said the voice that had spoken to Tyne. Paul turned back to the units he had just been looking over.

"Your presence at this point in space and time is unjustified within the symbolic structure of human society. Accordingly, your removal may now justifiably be effected."

Book Three: PATTERN

Emerging on that final plain,
Once more the watch-bell tolled again.
—Twice! Thor's soul and mine were one,
And a dragon shape had crossed the sun.

THE ENCHANTED TOWER

Chapter 17

"Set!" said Paul.

The word went out and was lost in the shadowy stillness above and behind the metallic shapes of the huge units standing over and around Paul. There was a slight noise behind him. He glanced toward it and saw a corridor opening once more in the general direction from which he had reached this area on the forty-ninth level. In the opposite direction a single unit slid out to fill most of the open space, and turned toward Paul. It rolled slowly toward him. He backed up and saw he was being forced into the newly opened corridor.

"So you can do violence to people," said Paul.

"No," said the voice that had spoken to Tyne. Now it seemed to come from the unit that was crowding Paul backward.

"You're doing violence to me right now."

"I am correcting a misplacement," said the voice. "Your value is external and false. It is perverting the symbological matrix of society at this moment."

122

"Nonetheless," said Paul, "you have a responsibility to me, as well as to society."

"More latitude," said the unit, forcing him back along the corridor, "is possible with those not sane, who are not responsible."

"I'm not sane?"

"No," said the machine, "you are not."

"I'd like," said Paul, "to hear your definition of sanity."

"Sanity," replied the voice, "in the human being is a response to natural instincts. It is sane to sleep, to eat, to seek to feed oneself, to fight if attacked, to sleep if no occupation is at hand."

Paul's shoulder blades came up against something hard. Turning around, he saw he had reached a turn in the corridor down which he was backing. The unit rolling toward him on invisible smooth-turning cylinders had not paused. He changed direction and backed away again.

"How about thinking? Is that sane?"

"Thought is a perfectly sane process, as long as it follows sane paths in the human brain."

"Such as those concerned with feeding and sleeping?"

"Yes."

"But not," said Paul, "those concerned with painting a picture or discovering a new method of interstellar travel?"

"Such thinking," said the unit, "is a response to abnormal irritations in the environment of the human concerned. Perfectly sane human beings have no need to do more than live and propagate, all under the conditions of greatest comfort."

"By those standards," said Paul, still backing up, "most of the human race is insane."

"You are quite wrong," said the voice, "roughly eighty-five per cent of the human race has had no real desire outside the framework I mentioned. Of the remaining fifteen, only about five in any generation have made any real effort to put their insanities into practice. Perhaps two per cent have some effect on future generations and one-tenth of one per cent are later admired even by the sane."

"I won't argue your figures," said Paul, feeling his left shoulder brush a unit, unyielding as the brick wall against which a man stands before a firing squad. "Even though I could. But don't you think the fact that your final category is admired even by the sane, as you put it, is some kind of an indication that maybe others had something besides insanity at work for them?"

"No," said the voice.

"Forgive me," said Paul. "I think I overestimated you. Let me say that again in terms you might be able to handle. Once you achieve an ideal existence for the human race, what's going to become of the arts, scientific research of all kinds, and the exploration of the natural universe?"

"They will be abandoned by the sane," said the machine.

Paul, backing up, saw the flanking units on either side of his corridor suddenly give way to open space. At the same time, the unit which had been herding him forward rolled level with the mouth of the corridor and stopped, so that Paul now found himslf facing a final wall. He turned and looked about him. He stood, completely hemmed in by a wall of units, upon the contact area at the end of the three-step accelerator. The end of the tube, the terminal that could tear him from this spot off into the universal ubiquity of no-time, loomed high above his head like a cannon mouth over the head of a sparrow which, in its muzzle, had taken refuge from a hawk.

"And the insane, at that time?" asked Paul.

"There will be no more insane," said the voice. "They will have destroyed themselves."

Paul saw nothing to give him any impression, and heard nothing; but deep within his flesh and bones he felt the accelerator warming to life. Even now, back and forth over flashing yards of distance, the point of no-time to be, was warming to life. Paul thought of Springboard, and of the emptiness of space.

"You tried to get me to destroy myself, didn't you?" said Paul, remembering what Jase had said. "In the mine; in front of the marching society that day."

"Always," said the voice, "the way has been open for you to destroy yourself. It is what works best with the insane. The sane are easy to kill. The insane fight very hard against being killed, but are more susceptible where it comes to the opportunities of self-destruction."

"Do you realize," asked Paul, feeling the accelerator warming to life over him, "your definition of sane and insane is completely artificial and wrong?"

"No," said the machine, "I cannot be anything but correct. It is impossible for me to be incorrect."

"You ought to see," said Paul, "that one false assumption used as a basis for later decisions could cause all your conclusions to be in error."

"I know this. I also know I contain no false assumptions," answered the voice. Above the looming curve of the accelerator the dusk of the dark higher up seemed to be pressing down on Paul. Almost, the voice seemed to descend also, becoming confidential. "My assumptions must stand the test of whether the structures built upon them guarantee a safe and continued life to mankind. This they do. I am humanity's guardian. You, in contrast, are it's destroyer."

"I——?" asked Paul, staring up into the darkness.

"I know you. You are the destroyer of mankind. You are the warrior who will not fight and cannot be conquered. You are proud," said the machine. "I know you, Necromancer. Already you have done incalculable damage, and created the first blind living form of the inconceivable enemy."

A barrier went down in Paul's mind. What was beyond it, he could not at this moment see; but it brought him relief and strength. It was as if a soldier, after long waiting, had at last received definite orders commanding him upon a long and desperate journey.

"I see," said Paul quietly, as much to himself as to the machine.

"To see is not enough," said the voice. "It is not enough excuse. I am the living wish of mankind expressed in solidity. I have the right to direct people. You have not. They are not yours. They are mine." The tones of the voice did not vary, but Paul got an impression of total effort being directed against him. "I will not let you lead mankind blindfold through a dark maze to an end they cannot conceive of, and final destruction. I cannot destroy you, or I would. But I can put you aside."

The voice paused slightly.

Paul was suddenly aware of a slight humming from the great cylinder head beside and above him. The acceleration was nearing the point of break into no-time which, like a sudden spark jumping, would contact and remove him from the point where he stood. He had just time to remember that he had been through no-time before, on the heels of Jase and Kantele when they escaped the police in the office across the concourse from the Koh-i-Nor. But that had been like running down a flight of stairs, while this would be like being thrown down them. He had just time to brace his awareness.

'*Now*," said the machine.

And Paul was ripped from the position he held in time and space and spread out to the uttermost reaches of the universe.

Chapter 18

Paul was not immediately delivered at the destination to which the machine had sent him.

From the psychic point of view the action of the accelerator upon him was like that of hurling him down an endless flight of infinitely stretching stairs. But even as he tumbled, that invincible part of him, like the reflexes of a superbly conditioned athlete, was instinctively gathering his feet under him, regaining his balance, and stopping his fall. It checked him, got him upright; but the conscious part of him was for the moment stunned and dazed, out of action. Instinctively in action, like a half-knocked-out fighter too well trained to stay down, he fought clear of the push of the accelerator and wandered, as it were, off sideways along one of the stair surfaces.

The situation was entirely different from when he had gone through no-time on the heels of Jase and Kantele, when he and they had been escaping the air police across from the Koh-i-Nor Hotel. The way by which they had entered no-time then, had been by a much more bearable emotional route. The accelerator method (lacking the medication that was yet to be discovered) was simply and plainly brutal.

It achieved its desired end by sheer savagery of action. It was this that had caused effects ranging from severe nervous breakdown to death in early Springboard volunteers transmitted to the terminal from which Paul had left. In essence, under the accelerator method, the individual's identity fled the immediate level of no-time to escape the suddenly intolerable conditions under which it had been forced to experience real time and space. Inanimate objects, of course, had no such difficulties. But the human psyche could not have retained its orientation under a full experiencing of conscious dispersal to universal dimensions and later reassembly. In instinctive self-protection it made the great step upward into the subjective universe.

Now, experiencing this, Paul suddenly understood the operation of the Alternate Laws, which were naturally entirely subjective in nature. However, at the moment this understanding could make no contact with the operative areas of his mind, which were still stunned. These wandered the subjective dimension of that line of endeavor to which the greater part of his being was dedicated.

There was no shape or dimension to the subjective universe in which he now wandered. It was, however, subject to the reality imposed on it by the symbolic processes of Paul's deeper self. Consequently, to him now, it took on the appearance of a vast, pebbled plain, with the pebbles growing in size in the distance. It was the plain of which he had dreamed on returning to the hotel after his first meeting with Jase.

Before, he had toiled over it as if walking. Now he skimmed rapidly just above its surface. Gray, black, rubbled, and bleak, the plain stretched off about him in all directions, not to any horizons, but to a great but finite distance. An emptiness of spirit, a sense of desolation, made up the atmosphere around him. He chilled in it, even while the unstunned part of him struggled to remind him that it was all subjective, all interpretative of the job he had, at a great distance in time and space, once dedicated himself to do.

"Arrogant," murmured a wind across the larger pebbles with the voice of Jase.

"These are my people, not yours," whispered a metallic breeze from another direction. And then, from a little farther off, and fainter even: *"I know you, Necromancer. . . ."*

He went quickly from the voices. The pebbles grew to boulders, to huge and mammoth shapes, to vast mountains with darkness between them. Then, at last, over the farthest and largest of these, he came to the final edge of the plain.

He went swiftly to it. From a point above the last and most mountainous boulder shapes he hung and looked down, out, and up at the same time upon a shifting infinity of darkness.

It was a gulf beyond which he felt there was light. But he could not see it, for the closer darkness. And in the darkness, something stirred.

It was barely living yet. It was an embryo, an amoeba, with only so much of consciousness as had allowed it to sense his existence when he had been under initiation, deep in the rock of Mercury. And only so much of reaction as had allowed it to make that one reactive, whiplash attack in his direction. It's growing was all yet before it.

And it was all in the way of evil that the Super-Complex had said it was. And Paul had created it. Without him it would never have been, but now it lived, and grew in power and understanding.

A terrible desire came over him then, to attack it now and settle the matter once and for all. But when he moved to go beyond the edge of his plain, he found something invisible there that would not let him pass. It was the barrier of the laws under which he had created what stirred out there. The laws that protected it from him as much as he from it, until the time when both he and it should be strong enough to break all barriers. And suddenly his dazed mind cleared, and he realized that if he should meet and conquer it now, nothing would be proved. Nothing accomplished. There would have been no point in its creation in the first place.

Abruptly, his mind was clear again. He retreated swiftly from the edge of the plain. He returned to the area where the boulders were again down to the size of pebbles. And here, close to where he had wandered astray, he found something like a cairn, or stony pile, new-built. It was about three times his own height, and the chance crevices between its stones gave an eerie impression of tiny arrow-slits or windows, though he felt instinctively that there was nothing alive about it as yet, nothing within. Standing beside it, he looked once more about the plain, and saw now that here and there at the farthest limits, this subjective landscape of his seemed to have elevated itself slightly, as if in the beginnings of hills, in a circle, surrounding him.

With that, he gave in to the original impulse that had brought him here and went forward to his destination.

He came to ordinary consciousness again in what looked like a small apartment. He had one brief glimpse of it before his legs—he had come through standing in the same position in which he had faced the Supe—crumpled under him and the full shock of what had been done to him took its price from his physical body. He pitched to the floor.

Here again, as always, he did not go completely under into unconsciousness. By all ordinary standards he should have gone completely out, but in actuality he only passed into a foggy, uncertain state which was the physical equivalent of his dazed condition while he had been wandering the subjective universe. During the succeeding several days in which this state gradually wore itself out, he was vaguely conscious of the fact that he had dragged himself from the floor to a nearby couch, and that he had once or twice drunk from a water dispenser that was nearby. Otherwise, he had not eaten or slept, or even fallen into the half-active dream-filled state that was his ordinary slumber.

He did not suffer in a physical sense. He had in no meaning of the term suffered any physical damage as a result of being transmitted to this spot. What had been torn about and attacked in him was his essential, immaterial identity. And the effect was similar to that of an attack of profound depression. He was perfectly capable physically of getting up and examining his surroundings.

The act of will required to do so, however, was like that of lifting his own body's weight to a man drained of blood almost to the point of death.

Gradually, however, he recovered.

He became aware first that the apartment was shaped like a section of a cylinder, its bottom curve having a floor built across it. It was fitted with the compact luxury of an ocean-going submersible liner. Between the curved walls were couch and easy chairs, tape cabinets, music player, bar, kitchen—even some finger-sculptures, and a couple of interesting stochastic paintings, one in oils, the other in red, black, and yellow clays.

There was also the cleared area, floored in polished black, which had been the terminal point of his arrival.

It was sometime on the third day that he found himself staring at the paintings, as he had for some hours now, like a man stupified. His feeble but certain perception made the connection immediately, and he laughed weakly. He had suddenly realized the existence of a plasma that could in part replace the psychic blood of which he had been drained.

He struggled wearily up from the couch and went clumsily on hands and knees across the room to the music player. From there he went to the tape cabinets, and to some adjoining shelves where he found a reference printer.

Twenty minutes later found him back on the couch. The fine, golden threads of *Il Trovatore* were spinning themselves out of the speakers of the music player, the rich canvas of Rubens' "Adoration of the Magi" was displayed in the tank of the tape cabinets, and the solemn heartbreak of Milton's sonnet on his blindness tolled like a slow and shadowed bell from a printer sheet in Paul's hand:

When I consider how my light is spent
Ere half my days in this dark world and wide . . .

Paul lay there, changing art, music, and poetry for mathematics, philosophy, medicine, and all the fields of man's endeavor. And slowly the life of those who had

had something to give to life seeped back into his own drained being, and his strength came back to him.

By the fourth day after his arrival he was back to normal. He got himself a large meal out of the kitchen, and then set about exploring the limits of this prison to which he had been sentenced.

It was about thirty feet in length, and about that same height and width at its greatest points of those two dimensions. Either end of it was a great circle flattened off at the bottom by the chord-line of the floor. One circle overlooked the terminal area of his arrival. The other merely filled up the far end of the living space.

It was this second circle that Paul looked over with interest. The first, overhanging the terminal point of his arrival, presumably simply hid the business end of an accelerator. The second might, however, be blocking the way to an escape route. When he looked closely, he discovered that the second in fact did appear to be something in the nature of a removable cover, held in place by a simple magnetic lock.

He unlocked the cover and the lower half of it swung away from him like half of a huge Dutch door. He walked through it and found himself in a farther extension of the cylinder, three times as big as the living quarters and filled with crated equipment and tools. He let his gaze settle over the tools and crates, and the answer he was looking for became easily apparent to him. This was the material with which the accelerator terminal here could be fitted to transmit as well as receive. He paused to glance at the tickets attached to some of the crates, but they were punch cards notated in a technician's shorthand that he did not know. He went on to the still farther circular wall that ended this division of the cylinder.

This had been sealed with a running bead of plastic weld all around its rim. It was evidently intended to be easily removed, but only by someone who knew how to do so, and why he was doing it.

Paul turned back and searched the second room once more, but there was no message or instruction list in sight.

He went back into the living quarters, and proceeded to make a methodical search of that area. He excavated drawers and investigated files and cabinets. There was no instruction sheet or manual. Evidently, whoever this place had been designed for had been expected to have that sort of information in his head. Paul was standing in the middle of the living-area floor and looking about for some hiding place he might have overlooked, when there was a sound from behind him, from the direction of the terminal area.

He looked. There on the bare and polished surface he saw a newssheet lying, still slightly curled from the printer. He went to it and picked it up.

For a moment he could not imagine what reason had caused the Supe to send it through to him. The headings of the various stories on the front page screamed of riots, panics, and earthquakes. Then, sliding his eye up one column and down the next in automatic speed-reading, Paul saw a small item: WORLD ENGINEER GIVEN EX-TRAORDINARY POWERS.

By an unprecedented world-wide register vote, the World Engineer yesterday was awarded authority to freeze the credit numbers and deny all Complex serv-ices to rioters and those suspected of disturbing the peace. The Complex-Major tabulated an almost in-conceivable 82 per cent of the total voting popula-tion, with 97.54 per cent of the total voting registering in favor of awarding the additional authority to the World Engineer.

A tiny item. But Paul frowned. Highly important it was, but that did not seem to him sufficient cause for the Supe to send him the newssheet. Nor—he glanced back at the other stories upon the front page—was the news of widespread emotional disturbances and rioting suf-ficient. The machine was not equipped to gloat, and sure-ly with Paul imprisoned here as he was, there could be no other reason for informing him about events he was powerless to have an effect upon.

Still puzzling, Paul opened the newssheet to its second and third pages. Then he saw it.

By some apparent freak mishap, the printer had failed to bring out the printing on these two pages otherwise than as an an unreadable blur, except for one item as small as the front-page item Paul had just frowned over. That one stood out as if framed.

DRONE LOST

The Complex-Major today noted the information that one of its Springboard drones, carrying automatic terminal receiving equipment to the planet known as New Earth, fourth world of the star Sirius, has suffered a malfunction of the directing system and been lost in space. This drone, which three days ago was noted as being in position to land shortly on New Earth, apparently missed its landing and has fallen beyond that planet under conditions of movement which will carry it out of the Sirian system. There can be no hope of reestablishing contact, notes the Complex-Major, or of recovery of the drone.

Paul dropped the newssheet and, spinning about, strode swiftly back into the farther room. Seizing a tool like a chisel, he attacked the plastic weld around the rim of the circular end wall. The plastic peeled up under his gouging and a thin edge of the metal was revealed. He forced the chisel edge in under the edge of the revealed metal. For a moment there was resistance, and then the chisel plunged through. There was a sudden whistling insuck of air past Paul's hand, the plastic weld cracked loose halfway around the rim, and the lower half spanged sharply on a deep bass note. Before Paul's eyes a horizontal crack ran across the metal, and the lower half of it broke clean from the top and fell into the room.

Paul caught it. It was a thin sheet of light magnesium alloy. He bent it inward and laid it flat on the floor. Then he stepped one step forward and looked out, through heavy glass.

Before him was a rolling landscape under a slightly yellowish sky, an atmosphere hazed with fine dust. Something like tiny, close-packed fern leaves covered the ground and grew thickly and a little larger about an occasional boulder or outcropping of granitic rock. Farther back were low, broad trees whose trunks and limbs looked as if they had been shaped out of dark, twisted cable. The brilliant white points of two Ao-type stars, so close they seemed at the moment to be swimming into each other, peered burningly through the dust haze and made the illumination for the day outside.

From the sight of these and the landscape they lighted —a landscape rich in promise for the yet infant science of terraforming—Paul had no difficulty making the connection between his present location and one of the worlds described in popular articles as destinations for the Springboard drones.

The double star in the sky out there could only be Sirius and its close companion. Which meant that this was New Earth, and the message of the newssheet the Supe had sent him was clear. Paul, and this drone in which he found himself imprisoned, had been deliberately and officially "lost" from the records.

For a moment Paul leaned his forehead wearily against the cool pane of the glass. The long palm and fingers of his single hand pressed uselessly against the glass' thick surface. Out there beyond its protection was, according to all official reports, an atmosphere suffocating with hydrogen sulphide. Behind him was crated equipment he had not the education and training to assemble.

Suddenly he stiffened. His hand slipped down from the glass and he raised his head to look sharply out through the transparency.

Leaning against a boulder on this alien world a little more than a dozen feet from the drone and incongruous against the small, carpeting ferns, was a heavy cane of dark wood; Walter Blunt's cane, one end of which was cracked and splintered as it would have been from being used to smash a human skull.

Chapter 19

"I see," said Paul quietly to the empty room and the landscape beyond the glass. "Of course."

It was like driving through a strange city at night and being convinced that north lay on your right hand. Then, suddenly, a chance-glimpsed street sign, some small but undeniable scrap of information, brings suddenly the undeniable orientation that places north on the left. Abruptly, silently, without real physical movement, the universe swaps ends and you realize that all this time you have been heading west, not east.

Suddenly the pattern about Paul had become clear and correct, down to the last detail.

It was Blunt, of course. As he had instinctively felt all along, it was Blunt—this man who would not turn and show his face openly and clearly—who was the demon. Paul spoke out loud again, but not to Blunt.

"Get me out of here," he said.

No, came an answer from deep inside him, from the invincible part in the back of his mind.

"You mean," asked Paul, "we end here, you and me? The two of us?"

No.

"Then——?"

There's only one of us.

"I see," said Paul again, quietly. "I should have known that."

I can do anything you want. But if I do, what's the use? We won't have found any way other than force. Our work will all have been wasted, as the living darkness we created beyond the boulders would have been wasted if you had killed it then, or if you kill it now, while it's ungrown. It's up to you now to find the different way.

"Not the machine's way," said Paul. "Not the way you moved me out of that office just behind Jase and Kantele that time? A different way than either of those?"

135

Yes.

"I don't know where to start."

Perceive. Recapitulate. Feel.

"All right," said Paul. He looked out at the cable trunks and limbs of the trees beyond the window, and at the cane. "There is only one thing common to both the objective and the subjective universe. This is identity."

Yes. Go on.

"The objective universe can be expressed in its lowest common denominators as an accumulation of identity isolates, both living and nonliving."

That's right.

"The isolates, however, in order to live—that is, to have function along the single dimension of the time line—must pass in and out of combinations which can be called sets."

Continue, Brother.

"The sets, in order to create the illusion of reality in objective time and space, must at all times arrange themselves into a single pattern. The pattern may vary, but it can't be abandoned or destroyed without also destroying or abandoning the illusion of reality."

Entirely correct. And very good for a partial identity that is restricted to reasoning by use of emotion and response. We can be proud of you. Go on. The next step?

Paul frowned.

"Next step?" he asked. "That's all."

Application.

"Application? Ah!" said Paul, suddenly. "Of course. The so-called Alternate Laws"—he glanced once more at the cane against the boulder beyond the window—"and the talents deriving from them are merely methods of altering the pattern so that the illusion of reality temporarily permits actions ordinarily not permitted." He thought for a second. "Blunt doesn't understand this," he said.

Are you certain of that?

Paul smiled a little in the empty silence of the room.

"That's my department, isn't it? Understanding."

I submit myself. Go on.

Paul hesitated.

"Is there more?" he asked.

You wanted to get out of here. You have perceived and recapitulated. From here on you leave me for your own territory. Feel.

Paul closed his eyes. Standing with the yellow light from outside showing faintly through his lids, he tried for a total contact with all that surrounded him—room, drone, planet, suns, space. It was like attempting to make some delicate last connection with blind fingers at arm's length, out of sight inside a piece of complicated equipment. Only, Paul's effort was completely nonphysical. He was reaching out to feel fully and correctly the great pattern of the objective universe, so that he could fit his own identity perfectly into pivot position within its structure.

For a moment he made no progress. For a fraction of a second he felt the completely stripped feeling of total awareness, but lacking even a single point of contact as he floated free, swinging into position. Then, suddenly, it was like the moment of orientation that had followed his seeing the cane beyond the glass, but much greater. And mixed with it the sensation of melting together, like but greater than that which had come to him to finish his interview with the psychiatrist Elizabeth Williams.

In one sudden moment of no-time, Paul and the invincible part of him fused irreversibly together.

It was as if he had stood on a narrow stage and suddenly, on all sides, great curtains had been raised, so that he found himself looking away in all directions to enormous distances. But now—alone.

"Ave atque vale," he said, and smiled a little sadly. "Hail and farewell." He turned back to the glass of the window. "Destruct," he said. "Of course. Blunt planted that for me, and in his own limited way, he was right."

Paul turned back to the tools behind him. He chose a heavy sledge hammer and took it to the window. His first blow bent the metal handle of the sledge but merely starred the glass. But his next blow sent the sledge crashing through and the whole wall of glass fell out in ruins.

He took three rapid steps toward the boulder where the cane leaned, as the acid, choking atmosphere numbed his sense of smell with the assault of its odor and filled his lungs. He reached the cane and seized it even as his eyesight began to sear and blur with tears. Almost, he

could hear Blunt chanting, as he had chanted in the
vision tank back there underground at Malabar Mine
while Paul watched.

"Destruct! The ultimate destruct! The creative destruct
that will rescue Man from being saved forever . . ."

Then Paul felt his knees strike the ground as he fell.
And with that his identity quit his body forever and left
it there, fallen and dying in the suffocation of the yet-
untamed atmosphere of the world which would be called
New Earth, with a splintered walking stick clutched in its
single fist.

Chapter 20

*Full twenty-fathoms times five, thy body lies. Of its
bones is ocean debris made. . . .*

Thirty miles due west of La Jolla, California, which is
a few miles up the coast line from San Diego, on a
sandy underwater plateau six-hundred-odd feet below the
surface of the ever-moving blue Pacific, Paul's bodiless
identity hovered above a skeleton of a man wrapped and
weighted with half-inch chain. This place had not been
his original intended destination, but he had detoured
here to settle a purely emotional point in his own mind.
Now, hovering above the chain-wrapped skeleton, he
sensed with relief that the body it once supported had
died a natural death. It was not that he doubted that
Blunt had been willing to murder to gain the results he
wanted. It was just that he wished the ledger sheet on
which he and Blunt were totaled up together and against
each other to be as clean as possible.

He left the white bones in the peace of their eternal
darkness, and went his way.

His way—the way Blunt's cane on New Earth had
been designed to send him—led him to an awakening in
something like a coffin. He lay, legs together, arms at
his sides, on his back, and tightly enclosed in a metal
container. His eyes were open but they saw nothing but

blackness. His pattern-linked perception, however, recognized that he was in a sort of cold-storage vault—something very like the slide-out six-and-a-half-foot drawers for unclaimed bodies in a public morgue. The body he now inhabited was identical with the one he was used to, except that it had two good arms. However, it seemed completely paralyzed.

It was paralyzed, he recognized with a sudden grim humor, because it was frozen stiff. The container in which he lay was surrounded with refrigerator coils and his body's temperature was a little more than twenty degrees below zero, Fahrenheit. The body would first have to be thawed before any life could be brought to it.

Paul surveyed the surrounding pattern. It would be surprising if Blunt, who had made so many arrangements where Paul was concerned, had not also made some here. Sure enough, the container lay on tilted tracks and was held inside the freezing unit by the bare hooking of a catch. Paul made the necessary slight alterations in the pattern and the catch failed. He slid out into the light of a brightly illuminated room without windows.

As he emerged into the room, the temperature rose sharply and suddenly from close to freezing to seventy-six degrees Fahrenheit. Lying at a tilted angle that put his feet close to the floor below the container and his head several inches higher, Paul saw it was a small room with a single door and no furniture, tiled in white.

The single item of interest in it was a message neatly printed in large letters on the wall opposite Paul. It read:

Paul: As soon as you find yourself able,
come and join us in suite 1243, at the Koh-i-Nor.
—Walt Blunt

Paul's container had gone into action on its own now. It was beaming deep, gentle heat into the very center of his frozen bones and tissues. It would take—what? Half an hour, perhaps longer, to bring him up to a living temperature so that his identity could take over command of this new body in the ordinary sense. Of course, almost undoubtedly Blunt had planned that Paul would help and hurry the process along. In any case it was

rather fine scheduling, and showed an attitude toward
other people and the universe that was far from modest.
For the first time—in such small unexpected ways,
thought Paul, do past things of minor importance explain themselves—Paul received a sudden extra insight
into Jase's repeated accusation of arrogance. Over the
years Jase must have become well acquainted with arrogance, in the person of Blunt.

Yes, thought Paul, he would hurry things along. But
in a way in which Blunt, with his less complete awareness of the patttern, could not expect. Blunt would not
expect that the message on the wall would be a clear
warning to Paul that the Chantry Guild had already
made its move. Outside this room the world would be
trapped in a war—a strange, weird war such as it had
never known before. And Blunt, general of the attacking
forces, would have timed the entrance of Paul upon the
battlefield for the most effective moment from Blunt's
point of view.

Only Paul would come early.

He reached into the pattern and to the invincible
knowledge that had become a part of him with his own
individual ability. He cut certain lines of casual relationship, and established new ones. The pattern altered, in the
immediate identity area of the body. And the body itself
floated upright out of its container.

It floated toward the door. The door opened. Skim-
ming just about the steps, it mounted a flight of stairs
and passed through a farther door into a small hallway.
Beyond, was a third door, a transparent door to the traffic level, on a street Paul recognized as being less than a
dozen blocks from the Koh-i-Nor. It was night beyond
this last door, and for some reason the Complex without
seemed darker than it should be.

Paul's body floated to the last door. It opened and he
floated out into the hot July night. The Complex Internal Weather Control seemed to have failed in its func-
tioning, for the temperature outside here was in the high
nineties at the very least and humidity must be close to a
hundred per cent. The still air of the Complex seemed
to hang heavily in the unusual shadows between struc-

tures, and its heat wrapped itself steamily around Paul's
icy body.

No vehicles were in motion. And here, at least, the
streets seemed deserted. Paul swung about and skimmed
off along the concrete walk in the direction which he
knew would take him to the Koh-i-Nor.

The streets were as empty as if the people in the Complex had locked and barred their doors against some
plague or roaming madness. In the first half block the
only sound Paul heard was the insane, insect-like buzzing of a defective street light. He looked up at its pulsat-
ing, uncertain glow, and saw at least part of the reason
it did not do well. Its pole had become a monstrous cane
of red-and-white striped candy.

Paul floated on. At the next corner he passed a closed
door. From the crack beneath it, however, a flood of red
fluid remarkably like blood in its color and viscosity was
flowing. One block farther on, Paul turned down into a
new street and saw his first living person of the night.

This was a man with his shirt half torn off, who was
sitting in a doorway and turning a kitchen knife over
and over in his hands. He looked up as Paul came toward
him.

"Are you a psychiatrist?" he said. "I need——" His
lifted eyes caught sight of Paul's feet and the space between them and the pavement. "Oh," he said. He looked
down at his hands and went back to playing with his
knife again.

Paul paused. And then he realized that his body could
not speak. He went on, and as he did so he reached
once more into the pattern. It was possible, as he had
suspected Blunt had intended, to hurry things up. Living
cells could not be thawed quite as crudely as dead meat,
but borrowing heat uniformly from the general surroundings was even more efficient than the deep-heating
mechanism of the storage container had been. Slowly,
but at the same time much more rapidly than might have
been expected, a living warmth came to Paul's body as he
proceeded on toward the Koh-i-Nor.

He passed other things of the night which bore little
relation to normality. A monument in the center of one

street crossing was slowly melting down as he passed,
like wax in a warm oven. The stone head of a lion, at the
corner of a heavy balcony running around one large
building, dipped its heavy muzzle and roared down at
him as he passed below. In the center of one street he
passed a circle of blackness—a hole of nothingness that
showed, not the level below, but a spatial distortion on
which the human eye was not equipped to focus. No cars
were running—Complex Transportation must have been
as inactive or powerless as Internal Weather—but occasionally Paul saw other people, alone, on foot, and at
some distance. None of them stayed to talk when they
saw him coming, but hurried off rapidly.

Life was rapidly taking over Paul's body. He had
started the heart early. By the time he reached the concourse his temperature was at ninety-six and a fraction of
a degree, pulse and respiration almost normal. He could
have walked it, but he waited until he actually reached
the entrance to the North Tower of the hotel before he
put his feet to the ground.

He walked into a dim-lit lobby illuminated only by
emergency lighting, and empty of guests. A white face
stared at him from well back of the desk counter. It was
the clerk with the elegant longhand. Paul paid him no
attention, but walked on around the corner to the elevators.

These, being a balanced system running on stored
power, had been unaffected by the obvious curtailment
of services otherwise. Silently, gently, efficiently, as if the
human race were already dead and only a mechanical
duty remained, the disks floated one after another in regular, spaced intervals, up and down the transparent
tubes of their shafts. Paul stepped onto a disk ascending
the up shaft.

He slid smoothly up, past a succession of empty hall-
ways, barely lighted by the red emergency light above the
door to the stairs on each level. Only once did he see
someone. That was in passing the ninth level. It was a
woman—a young woman, almost a girl. At the sight of
him passing up the elevator tube, she turned hastily and
ducked into a doorway.

He went on up.

The twelfth level of the hotel, in contrast to the rest of the world Paul had seen that night, was fully lighted. Its illumination seemed almost garish in contrast to the surrounding dark. But no one stirred about its corridor, either. More than this, Paul received from the closed doors he passed an impression of darkness and emptiness beyond, as if suite 1243 toward which he walked was the only space with life within it on this bright level.

When he turned a last corner of the corridor and approached 1243, he saw its door was ajar. It stood three-quarters of the way rolled back into its wall socket, and the sound of a voice came audibly through the opening.

The voice was that of Kirk Tyne.

". . . your blind spot," he was saying. "That's what I can't understand, Walt. A man of your intelligence who thinks the present can be changed *in* the present, without going back and altering the predisposing factors of the past. And so you let loose this madness on the world."

Paul stopped just short of the entrance. He had heard this argument from Tyne before, at the time when Tyne had taken him onto the World Engineer's personal staff. Now it struck Paul as interesting to know what Blunt's answer to it would be.

"You've sold your birthright for a mess of circuits," answered Blunt's voice. "You don't think, Kirk. You parrot what the Supe tells you. If the past can't be changed, the present must. For the future's sake."

"Will you use a little logic?" asked Tyne. "I tell you the present *cannot* be changed without changing the past. Even the Supe, with all its stored knowledge, wouldn't be able to calculate the ultimate possibilities of a single insect's life pattern being altered in the past. And that's the easier way. What you're trying here, now, tonight, is the harder."

"Kirk," said Blunt's voice. "You're a fool. The predisposing factors leading up to this hour have been laid and set up for centuries now. All that's necessary for us is to recognize them and use them."

"I tell you that's not true!"

"Because your Supe . . ." Blunt was beginning, with hard irony forming a cutting edge to his resonant voice, when Paul stirred himself again. He stepped forward, entered the doorway, and walked into the main lounge of what was probably one of the best suites the Koh-i-Nor had to offer its guests.

Around this large room seven people stood in tableau. Close and on Paul's left was Kantele. Just beyond her, half turned away from the entrance, was Blunt, an odd tall hat on his head and a heavy black cape with purple facings rippling down from his wide shoulders. Beyond Blunt stood Burton McLeod, who of all seven showed the least concern, and Jase, also in cape and hat. His back to the blue curtains closed across the wide, far window wall of the room opposite the door, stood Eaton White, like a small, colorless silhouette. To White's left, on the opposite side of the room, stood the Koh-i-Nor Hotel's security agent, James Butler. But the bizarre touch was upon him, too. He wore the all-black jumper and slacks of one of the better-known marching societies, an outfit that left only face and hands whitely exposed; and in one of those white hands, he held a slim, lethal police handgun which had had its front sight removed. In place of the sight gleamed a small, blue metal cross.

He and McLeod stood across from each other with perhaps a dozen feet of carpet between them. The police handgun casually covered the chest of McLeod, and both men stood untensely, but as if aware of no others in the room besides themselves.

Closest of all, on Paul's right, stood Tyne. He faced the half-turned-away Blunt, and so was, like the colorless and motionless Eaton White, the first to see Paul as he entered. The sudden widening of his eyes made Blunt check his speech. The rest all turned, even Butler and McLeod. And Kantele gasped. They, all except Blunt, stood like people who witness a basic violation of the natural laws by which they have lived all their lives.

But Blunt leaned upon the straight silver knob of a new walking stick and smiled. As perhaps the Athenian polemarch Callimachus smiled on that day in late September, twenty-five hundred and forty years previous, on seeing in the cool bright sunlight between clouds, the dust of his reinforced Greek wings close in on the Persian horde on the plain of Marathon.

"You're a little early, not too much," he said, looking

at Paul. "Kirk here hasn't quite been softened up enough yet. But come on in—myself."

And Paul, walking into the suite, seeing Blunt full and clearly face on for the first time, saw indeed—himself.

Chapter 21

Paul strode into the suite. The eyes of all of them were fixed on him, but none showed more shattering from the blow than the blue eyes of Kantele. For, of course, she alone of them all had felt it from the beginning, even though she would not admit it to herself. It was the reason she had been so drawn to Paul, and had denied being drawn so fiercely. Paul had not blamed her then; and understanding as he did now, he blamed her less. Even for him, as he stopped, facing Blunt from the distance of a few feet, the experience had its unnatural elements.

To those standing watching, he knew, it must be worse. For it was not a physical resemblance that he shared with Walter Blunt. They were both tall, wide-shouldered, long-boned, with strong facial features. But there the similarity of the flesh ceased. Their common identity was all the more jolting to the emotions because it was a matter of non-physical duplications. They should not have looked alike. But they did.

It was weirdly as if the same man wore two different costumes and disguises. The surface appearances were totally different, but identically the same way of standing, the same balance of movement, the same mannerisms and attitudes, glowed through the outer shells like the same candle-flame through two differently ornamented lanterns.

"You understand," said Blunt conversationally to Paul, "why I've dodged you all this time?"

"Of course," said Paul.

At that, Kirk Tyne finally found his voice again. And a note that rang clearly in it witnessed to the fact that for the first time the World Engineer was seriously shaken in his convictions.

"What kind of unnatural devil-thing is this, Walt?" he burst out.

"It's a long story," said Blunt. He still leaned on his cane, examining Paul almost the way a connoisseur might examine a particularly valued work of art. "But that's what I brought you here to hear, Kirk."

Kirk glanced from Paul to Blunt and back, as if magnetically attracted against his will.

"I don't believe it," he said.

"Neither the world nor I," answered Blunt, without shifting his gaze off Paul, "will care what you think after tonight, Kirk."

"Satan!" said a voice. Those in the room, including Paul and Blunt, all looked. It was James Butler, the hotel agent, and he was lifting the gun in his hand. The blue cross on the end of its barrel centered on Paul, wavered, and swung over to point at Blunt. "Denier of God."

Something black flickered through the air of the room. There was the sound of a soft impact, and Butler staggered and dropped the gun from his suddenly limp grasp. The polished haft of a leaf-shaped, hiltless knife stood out from the muscles of the agent's shoulder. McLeod came walking calmly across the room. He bent to scoop up the gun and tucked it into his waistband, and then taking hold of Butler's shoulder with his left hand, he pulled out the knife with his right. He pulled a self-adjusting pressure bandage from his pocket, put it around Butler's shoulder to cover the wound, and lifted the crippled arm across Butler's chest into the grasp of Butler's other arm.

"Hold that," he said. Butler looked at him. The agent had not made a sound. McLeod went back to his position beyond Blunt.

"Now," asked Kirk, out of a white face, "you sick your hoods on me, and decent people?"

"You call that fanatic decent?" asked Blunt, nodding at the black-clad Butler. "How decent would he have been if he'd shot me, or Paul? As he would have, if Burt hadn't stopped him."

"It makes no difference," said Kirk. Before their eyes,

with a remarkable effort of will, they saw the man pull himself together. He repeated himself more calmly. "It makes no difference. None of this makes any difference. There are still only sixty thousand of you. That's not enough to wreck the world."

"Kirk," said Blunt, "you know I enjoy arguing with you. You make such a fine straight man."

"The credit goes to you as the comic," said Kirk, dryly.

"Now, that's more like it," said Blunt, nodding his head thoughtfully. "You see, Kirk, I want to break you. If I can get you nicely broken, I can enlist you in tearing this civilization up by the roots and get it done twice as fast. Otherwise, I wouldn't waste time talking with you like this."

"I assure you," said Kirk, "I don't feel the least bit broken."

"You aren't supposed to—yet," said Blunt.

"All I see so far," said Kirk, "is a series of adult-scale Halloween tricks."

"For example?" asked Blunt. "Paul, here?"

Kirk glanced at Paul and for a moment hesitated.

"I don't believe in the supernatural," he said.

"Nor do I," said Blunt. "I believe in the Alternate Laws. Under their power, I created Paul. Didn't I, Paul?"

"No," said Paul. "Creation isn't that easy."

"I beg your pardon," said Blunt. "Let me put it this way then—I built you. I brought you to life. How much do you remember?"

"I remember dying," said Paul. "I remember a tall figure wearing the cape and hat you're wearing now, who brought me back to life."

"Not brought you back," said Blunt. "The real Paul Formain is dead—you knew that?"

"I know it now," said Paul. "I investigated."

"I had tracers on a number of youngsters like him for over fifteen years," said Blunt, "waiting for an opportunity. Odds were with me. Sooner or later one was bound to die under convenient conditions."

"You could have rescued him from that sailboat while he was still alive," said Paul.

"I could have," said Blunt. He looked squarely at Paul.

"I think you know why I wouldn't do such a thing. I got to him in time for the moment of his death. I got several cells from his body, living cells. Under the powers of the Alternate Laws, I regrew from each of those cells a living body."

"More?" ejaculated Kirk, staring in something like horror at Paul. Blunt shook his head.

"Living," he said, "but not alive, any more than the dying body I took them from was alive in the true sense. The conscious personality of a living human being is something more than an arithmetical total of the consciousness of its parts." He gazed at Paul for a second without speaking, then said slowly, "Under the Alternate Laws I sparked his life with a portion of my own."

There was a silence in the room, so complete that it seemed that for a moment everyone there had ceased breathing.

"I made another *me,*" said Blunt. "His body, his memories, his skills were those that belonged to the boy who had just died. But in essence, he was me."

"In one essence," corrected Paul, "I was you."

"The most important essence, then," said Blunt. "That was why your body wouldn't take an arm graft. Your body's cells had used up their ability to make large adjustments and repairs in forming you."

"He has two arms now," said Kirk.

"This isn't the original body I started him in," said Blunt. "I assume he had to leave the first one on New Earth?" He looked inquiringly at Paul.

"By your cane," said Paul.

"Yes," said Blunt. "That cane."

"What cane?" asked Kirk.

"The cane that killed Malorn," said Paul. He gazed with a still face at Blunt. "The cane with which *he* killed Malorn."

"No," said McLeod, from behind Blunt. "I did it. It took someone who knew how to handle it like a singlestick. Walt just twisted the Alternate Laws to let me do it."

"But why?" cried Kirk. "Murder, canes, New Earth! I don't understand." He stared. "To educate Paul in———" He broke off.

"You're breaking very nicely, Kirk," said Blunt, turning his head briefly toward the World Engineer and then coming back as always to look at Paul. "You see how little you know? Even your Supe didn't inform you that it had used the accelerator down in its guts to ship Paul off to a planet circling Sirius and its companion star. I'll tell you the rest now and we'll see how you stand up to it." He nodded at the curtained window. "Open that," he said to Eaton White.

The colorless little man hesitated.

"Go ahead," said Kirk, harshly.

White reached in among the folds of the curtains, and down. They drew back revealing a wall-wide window above a low ledge about two feet high.

"All the way," said Blunt.

White reached and pressed again. The whole window slid down into and through the ledge. The hot air of the steamy night outside welled into the conditioned coolness of the room.

"Look!" said Blunt. "Listen out there." He pointed with his stick at the bulking darkness of the Complex outside, lighted here and there dimly. On the hot still air came the sound of chanting, the *"Hey-ha! Hey-ha!"* of a marching society. And from closer by, out of sight somewhere twelve stories below the window ledge, came a long drawn-out howl from something human that had gone a long ways back toward the animal.

"Look," said Blunt. Turning, he threw his cane out the window. Wheeling, spinning about the axis of its center point, the two rotating ends blurred themselves into scalloped, raking wings. The center acquired a rodent body, and a bat-shape instead of what had been a stick beat upward blackly against the dim glow of the Complex, turned and swooped back, gliding into the room to end up a stick in Blunt's hand again.

"Sixty thousand, you said," said Blunt to Kirk. "The unstable groups, organizations, and elements in this world of ours total nearly one-fifth the world population. For forty years the Chantry Guild has primed them for this moment of final breakdown. One-fifth of the world is out of its senses tonight, Kirk."

"No," said Kirk. "I don't believe it. No, Walt."

"Yes, Kirk." Blunt leaned on his cane again. His dark

eyes under the eaves of his aging eyebrows bored in on
the other man. "For centuries now you and your kind
kept the hound of Unreason chained and locked away
from the world. Now we've set him loose again—loose
for good. From now on, there'll be no certainty to existence. From now on there'll always be the possibility that
the invariable laws won't work. Reason and past experience and the order of the community will fail as
guides, and the individual will be left with nothing to
anchor to, only himself."

"It won't work," said Kirk. "Those streets out there
are mostly empty. We moved too fast for you, my staff
and the Super-Complex. Lack of light, lack of comfort,
lack of services—people are hiding in their rooms now,
because we forced them there. They can only hide so long;
then the basic needs—hunger, reaction against boredom
—will take over. They'll come out in the daylight and see
how little your Halloween tricks have changed the essential structure of their lives. They'll adjust and learn
to live with the necessarily small percentage of your
magic in the same way they live with the small possibilities of other freak accidents or being struck by
lightning."

"*You* moved too fast!" said Blunt. "You only reacted
with all the fine obedience of one of your machines.
The streets are dark because I wanted them that way.
The heat is driving people to huddle apart from each
other, alone with their fears, each in his own room, because these are the best breeding grounds for Unreason.
Tonight is not something to which people can become
accustomed, it's only the first battle in a war that will
go on and on, waged with new weapons, fought in different ways, waged on altering battlefields, until you and
your kind are destroyed."

Blunt's hard old jaw lifted.

"Until the final moment of destruct!" His voice rang
through the room and out into the night. "Until Man is
forced to stand without his crutches. Until his leg irons
are struck off him and the bars he has built around him
are torn down and thrown away! Until he stands upright and alone, free—*free* in all his questioning, wandering spirit, with the knowledge that in all existence

there are only two things: himself, and the malleable universe!"

Blunt's heavy shoulders swayed forward over the cane on which he leaned, almost as if he was about to leap on Kirk Tyne where he stood. The World Engineer did not retreat before Blunt's words, or that movement, but he seemed to have shrunk slightly and his voice was a trifle hoarse when he answered.

"I'm not going to give in to you, Walt," he said. "I'll fight you to the bitter end. Until one of us is dead."

"Then you've lost already," said Blunt, and his voice was almost wild. "Because I'm going on forever." He pointed aside at Paul. "Let me introduce you, Kirk, to a younger, stronger, greater man than yourself, and the continuing head of the Chantry Guild."

He stopped speaking, and as the sound of his voice ceased, a sudden violent silence like summer sheet lightning flashed across the room. On the heels of it came an abrupt, instinctive, inarticulate cry from Jase.

"No," said Paul, "it's all right, Jase. The Guild will go to you. My job is something different."

They stared at him.

"Something different?" asked Blunt, dryly. "What is it *you* think you're going to do?"

Paul smiled at him and at the others a little sadly.

"Something brutal and unfair to you all," he said. "I'm going to do nothing."

Chapter 22

For a moment they merely looked back at him. But in that moment something inevitable, and not at all unique, happened. It has taken place before at gatherings that those present arrange themselves in a social pattern oriented around the strong point of one individual present. Then, something is said or something takes place. And suddenly, though none present have made an actual movement, the strong point is displaced to a different individual. The pattern reorients itself, and though nothing physical has happened, the emotional effect of the reorientation is felt by everyone in the room.

So with Paul, at that moment. He had reached out and touched the pattern, and like one drop melting into another, abruptly he was the focus for the emotional relationships in the room, where Blunt had been, a moment before.

He met Blunt's eyes across the little distance that separated them. And Blunt looked back, without expression, and without speaking. He leaned still on his cane, as if nothing had taken place. But Paul felt the sudden massive alertness of Blunt's genius swinging to bear completely on him, in the beginnings of a recognition of what Paul was.

"Nothing?" asked Jase, breaking the silence. Sudden alarm for the Chantry Guild, in this breakdown of whatever Blunt had planned for it, was obvious upon Jase, obvious even to others in the room besides Paul.

"Because," said Paul, "if I do nothing, you'll all go your separate ways. The Chantry Guild will continue and grow. The technical elements in civilization will continue and grow. So will the marching societies and the cult groups. So"—Paul's eyes, ranging backward in the room, met for a moment with Burton McLeod's—"will other elements."

"You want that to happen?" challenged Tyne. *"You?"*

"I think it's necessary," said Paul, turning to the World Engineer. "The time has come when mankind must fragment so that his various facets may develop fully and unaffected by other facets nearby. As you yourself know, the process has already started." Paul looked over at Blunt. "A single strong leader," said Paul, "could halt this process temporarily—only temporarily, because there would be no one of his stature to replace him when he was dead—but even in temporarily halting it, he could do permanent damage to later development of fragments he didn't favor."

Paul looked back at Kirk. There was something like horror on Kirk's face.

"But you're saying you're *against* Walt!" stammered Kirk. "You've been against him all along."

"Perhaps," said Paul, a little unhappily, "in a sense. It'd

be kinder to say that I haven't been *for* anyone, including Walt."

Kirk stared at him for a moment, still with an expression varying from shock almost to repugnance.

"But *why?*" Kirk burst out finally. *"Why?"*

"That," said Paul, "is a little hard to explain, I'm afraid. Perhaps, you might understand it if I used hypnosis as an example. After Walt first brought that last body of mine to consciousness, I had quite a period in which I didn't really know who I was. But a number of things used to puzzle me. Among them the fact that I couldn't be hypnotized."

"The Alternate Laws———" began Jase, from back in the room.

"No," said Paul. "I think someday you Chantry people are going to discover something to which your Alternate Laws bear the same relation alchemy does to modern chemistry. I couldn't be hypnotized because the lightest form of hypnosis requires the giving up of a certain portion of the identity, just as does really complete unconsciousness, and this is impossible to me." He looked around at all of them. "Because, having experienced a shared identity with Walt, it was inevitable that I should come to the capability of sharing the identity of any other human with whom I came in contact."

They all looked back at him. With the exception of Blunt, he saw, they had not fully understood.

"I'm talking about understanding," he said, patiently. "I've been able to share identities with all of you, and what I've found is that each one of you projects a valid form of the future of human society. But a form in which the others would emerge as stunted personalities if they managed to live in it at all. I can't further any one of these futures, because they'll all be coming into existence."

"All?" asked Kirk, just as, at the same moment, Jase also asked, "All?"

"You, yourself, were aware of the situation, Kirk," said Paul. "As you told me yourself, society is going through a necessary stage of fragmentation. It's only a matter of time, now, until a medication is devised that makes Springboard's work into the basis of a practical transportation system. As people spread out to the stars, the fragmentation will be carried further."

He stopped speaking to let that point sink in.

"None of you," said Paul, "should be wasting time fighting each other. You should be busy hunting up your own kind of people and working with them toward your own separate future."

He paused, to give them a chance, this time, to answer. No one seemed disposed to do so. And then, from perhaps the most unexpected quarter, came the protest.

"There's no reason to believe any of this," said Eaton White, in his thick, dry voice from beside the open window.

"Of course not," said Paul reasonably. "If you disbelieve me, you only have to have the courage of your convictions and ignore what I've said." He looked around at them all. "Certainly you don't believe I'm trying to talk you into anything? All I want to do is step out of the picture and go my own way, and I should think the rest of you would want to do likewise."

He turned back to meet Blunt's eyes.

"After all," he said, "this has been a transition period in history, as Kirk has, no doubt, often told other people besides myself. It's been a time of stress and strain, and in such times things tend to become dramatic. Actually, each generation likes to think of itself as at the pivot point in history, that in its time the great decision is made which puts man either on the true road or the false. But things aren't really that serious. Truthfully, the way of mankind is too massive to be kinked, suddenly; it only changes direction in a long and gradual bend over many generations."

Paul turned to the World Engineer.

"Kirk," he said, "as I say, I'm not trying to convince anyone. But certainly *you* can see I'm talking sense?"

Kirk Tyne's head came up with decision.

"Yes," he said sharply, "I can." He looked at Blunt and back to Paul. "Everything you say makes sense. Everybody has one person who can put the Indian sign on them. With me it's always been Walt." He turned to Blunt. "Because I always admired you, Walt. I wanted to believe in you. And as a result you were able to con me into thinking that the world was upside down and just about to be inside out. It took someone with his feet on the ground, like Paul here, to bring me back to Earth. Of course, our centuries-old technical civilization wasn't the sort of thing that could be hoodooed out of existence by black magic overnight. But you almost had me thinking it could."

He stepped up to Paul and held out his hand. Paul took it.

"Everybody owes you a lot," said Kirk, shaking Paul's hand. "But I, most of all. I want you to know I haven't any doubts where you're concerned. I'll get the services back in action immediately. Come on, Eat." He turned to Blunt, hesitated, shook his head, and turning away again, walked toward the door. Blunt smiled grimly after him.

Eaton White came forward from his position at the window. As he passed by Paul, he hesitated, turned to Paul, and opened his mouth as if to speak. Then he turned and went on out, after Kirk.

"Jim," said Paul gently, looking across at the black-clad hotel agent, still holding his helpless arm across his chest with his other hand, "you probably have responsibilities calling."

Butler snapped his head around at the sound of his first name like a man coming out of a dream. His eyes were like gun-muzzles trained on Paul.

"Yes," he interrupted. "Responsibilities. But not the sort you think. You've been the instrument of a revelation to me—the revelation of the New Jerusalem. The future may hold more than many think."

He turned and walked upright away, still holding his arm, until he passed through the door, and turning, vanished.

"Good-by, Walt," said a voice. Paul and Kantele turned to see that McLeod had come up and put his hand on Blunt's shoulder. Blunt, still leaning on his cane, turned his face sideways toward that hand.

"You, too?" he asked a little huskily.

"You'll be all right, Walt," said McLeod. "Truth is, I've been thinking of it for some time."

"For the last six weeks—I know," said Blunt with a

wolf's grin. "No, no, go on, Burt. There's nothing to stay here for now, anyway."

Burt squeezed the caped shoulder, looked across it compassionately at Paul, and went toward the door. The three who were left watched him out in silence.

When Burt had gone, Blunt swung about a little on his cane and looked sardonically at Paul.

"Do I have to love you, too?" he asked.

"No," said Paul. "No, of course not! I wouldn't ask that."

"Then, damn you," said Blunt. "Damn you and may you rot in hell until judgment day!"

Paul smiled sadly.

"You won't tell me why?" asked Blunt.

"If I could," said Paul, "I would. But it's a matter of language. I don't have words for you." He hesitated. "You could take it on faith."

"Yes," said Blunt, suddenly and heavily as if the strength had gone out of him. "I could take it on faith, if I were bigger." He straightened up suddenly and looked with a deep, penetrating curiosity at Paul.

"*Empath*," he said. "I should have suspected it sooner. But where did the talent come from?"

"From your plans for me," said Paul. "I told the truth. It's a high wall that separates the inner parts of one identity from the inner being of another. From having the experience of no wall between you and me, I could learn to tear down the walls between myself and all others."

"But why?" said Blunt. "Why would you want to?"

Paul smiled again.

"Partly," he said, "because unlimited power or strength is a little like credit. In the beginning it seems that enough of it would do anything. But, when you achieve it, you find that it, too, is limited. There are areas in which it's helpless, like other things. Can you hammer out a roughness in a delicate piece of carved jade?"

Blunt shook his head.

"I don't see how it applies," he said.

"It's just that I have some things in common," said Paul. "And Kirk was very nearly right. It's not possible to change the future except by changing the present.

And the only way to change the present is to return to the past and change that."

"Return?" asked Blunt. "Change?" Blunt's eyes had lost their earlier hardness. They were now fully alive. He leaned on his cane and looked directly at Paul. "Who could change the past?"

"Perhaps," said Paul, "someone with intuition."

"Intuition?"

"Yes. Someone," Paul said, "who could see a tree in a garden. And who knew that if that tree were to be cut down, then some years in time and some light-years in distance away, another man's life would be changed. A man, say, who has conscious intuitive process and can immediately realize all the end possibilities of an action the moment he considers it. Someone like that could step back into time, perhaps, and make changes without risk of error."

Blunt's face was perfectly still.

"You aren't me, at all," Blunt said. "You never were me. I think it was you who animated Paul Formain's body, not me at all. Who are you?"

"Once," said Paul, "I was a professional soldier."

"And an Intuit?" asked Blunt. "And now an Empath as well?" His voice was a little harsh. "What next?"

"An identity," said Paul slowly, "needs to be a dynamic, not a static, quantity. If it is static, it becomes helpless within the pattern of its existence. This is a lesson man eventually will have to learn. But if it is dynamic, it may direct its existence as a mining machine is directed, through the otherwise impassible fusion of rocky elements known as reality. From being dominated and imprisoned by them, it can pass to dominating and making use of them, and with its existence plow through, pulverize, and handle reality until it separates out those uniquely real and valuable parts of it which the identity wishes to make its own."

Blunt nodded, slowly, like an old man. It was not clear whether he had understood and was agreeing, or whether he had given up the attempt to understand and was merely being agreeable.

"They all would have their futures," he said. "That's what you told them, wasn't it?" He stopped nodding and looked at Paul for the first time with eyes that were a little faded. "But not me."

"Of course, you," said Paul. "Yours was the greatest vision, and simply the one furthest from realization, that was all."

Blunt nodded again.

"Not," he said, "in my lifetime. No."

"I'm sorry," said Paul. "No."

"Yes," said Blunt. He took a deep breath and straightened up. "I had plans for you," he said. "Plans rooted in ignorance. I had everything set up for you." He glanced at Kantele. "It was almost like having a——" He checked himself, threw back his head, and took a firmer grip on his cane. "I planned to retire after tonight, anyway."

He started to turn away. As he turned, he stooped a little. He hesitated and looked back at Kantele. "I don't suppose. . . . No," he said, interrupting himself. He straightened up once again, so straight the cane merely brushed the surface of the rug underfoot. He threw back his shoulders and for a moment towered in the room, as if he were young again.

"It's been an education," he said, and saluted Paul with the cane. Turning, he strode out. Behind his back, Kantele made a little gesture after him with her hands, and then let her hands and gaze drop. She stood, her head bent, her eyes on the carpet at her feet, like a maiden, captive to the stranger's bow and spear.

Paul looked at her.

"You love him," he said.

"Always. Very much," she said, almost inaudibly, not looking up.

"Then you're a fool to stay," he said.

She did not answer that. But after a moment she spoke again, uncertainly, her gaze still on the carpet.

"You could be mistaken," she said.

"No," said Paul; and she did not see the centuries-old pain that came into his eyes as he said it. "I never make mistakes."